James looked as though his night had been as bad as hers

"Last night was a mistake on my part—a human, stupid, male mistake. I've never pretended bogus feelings to get a woman to bed, and certainly not with you. But you *are* an alluring, desirable woman, and I wanted to make love to you."

"I can't accept your overtures at face value," Flora said bluntly. "Not that I don't find them attractive," she added, "because I do. But then something creeps in to remind me that possibly this is part of your plan to get Inch Cottage back."

"Do you really think I was trying to seduce you into giving up the tenancy?" James demanded.

"Well, *weren't* you?"

Catherine George was born in Wales and, following her marriage to an engineer, lived in Brazil for eight years at a gold-mine site. It was an experience she would later draw upon for her books, when she and her husband returned to England. Now her husband helps manage their household so that Catherine can devote more time to her writing. They have two children—a daughter and a son—who share their mother's love of language and writing.

LAWFUL
POSSESSION
Catherine George

Harlequin Books

**TORONTO • NEW YORK • LONDON
AMSTERDAM • PARIS • SYDNEY • HAMBURG
STOCKHOLM • ATHENS • TOKYO • MILAN
MADRID • WARSAW • BUDAPEST • AUCKLAND**

ISBN 0-373-15556-5

LAWFUL POSSESSION

CHAPTER ONE

IN THE summer heat the journey north seemed endless. When the train finally arrived at Glasgow Central Flora felt tired and travel-stained as she hurried for the bus which shuttled passengers to Queen Street Station for the con-nection to Mallaig. But she soon revived in the holiday atmosphere of the last lap of her journey. So many hikers and cyclists and tourists of all kinds were on board that it was no mean feat to smile and squeeze her way to her reserved seat, by which time the train was already emerging from the domed glass of the station into the sunlit July evening to take her by way of Dumbarton and Craigendoran to join the West Highland line.

Her weariness forgotten, Flora craned her neck from side to side, eager to see as much of the magnificent scenery as possible as the little train left the urban sprawl behind and began to skirt lochs and snake round horseshoe bends on its laborious way up to Rannoch Moor.

Delighted with such fine weather for her first view of the Highlands, Flora sat enthralled throughout the long, leisurely journey as the train crossed the moorland wilderness of peat bog and streams and tiny lochs then swooped down past Loch Taig and finally westward into Lochaber, where Ben Nevis loomed into view at last with evening sunlight glinting on the snow garlanding its massive, craggy summit. When the train pulled into Fort William Flora stretched her cramped limbs, hauled her bags from the train and made for the entrance, where to her relief a rangy, sandy-haired man in a tweed jacket came forward to relieve her of her luggage.

'You will be Miss Blair,' he stated. 'I am Donald MacPhail from Ardlochan.'

Flora shook his hand warmly. 'How do you do? It's very kind of you to meet me.'

Donald MacPhail, reserved, but not un-friendly, assured her courteously it was no trouble at all. As he drove her from the pleasant little town of Fort William he pointed out various places of interest *en route*, commenting on her good fortune at seeing Ben Nevis bathed in sun on her very first visit.

'Very true!' agreed Flora, smiling. 'My great-aunt said it was an entire week before she saw the summit her first time here.'

The ensuing silence was somewhat dampening. Was mention of her dead relative taboo? If so it could prove a trifle awkward, one way and another.

'The house is ready for you, Miss Blair,' said Donald, after a pause. 'Jean—my wife—has stocked the larder with food, and the bed is aired in the room Miss Lyon used.' He gave her a rather shy glance. 'We were sorry to hear she'd passed away.'

Flora thanked him gravely, grateful for his tact when he changed the subject.

They had driven some distance before Donald turned off on a narrow private road lined with drifts of fireweed and foxgloves dyed vermilion by the sunset light against their backdrop of forest green. Excitement, sharp and unexpected, rose in Flora as she caught her first glimpse of sky-tinted water which gradually revealed itself as a small loch with a dramatic glimpse of Ben Nevis in the far distance.

The view was familiar enough to Flora from the water-colour which hung over her bed at home, but seeing it for herself at first hand was vastly different. Her excitement mounted as the road skirted the loch, giving her a view of wooded shore which reached out in small pointed headlands into the water at intervals and gave, gradually in some places, sharply in others, to the lower slopes of hills, with higher mountain peaks beyond them in the distance. Across the loch she could see a group of tiny lights, just visible against the darkening sky. Their friendly pin-point glimmer only emphasised the isolation of the scene, but far from depressing Flora it cast a spell which grew stronger with every mile. Her anticipation was intense as Donald turned off on a track which led past outcroppings of rock through dense woodland, bringing her at last to a clearing, and a house with a panoramic view of the loch.

Donald nodded in confirmation when Flora looked at him, amazed. The house was so much larger than the but and ben of her imaginings that she was dumbfounded. Inch Cottage was no cottage at all, but a long, low, graceful building, with grey slate roof and white-painted stone walls sheltered by a glade of trees, with clumps of broom providing great splashes of yellow against the green.

Flora turned back to Donald blankly. '*This* is Inch Cottage?'

He permitted himself a faint, amused smile. 'Yes, indeed, Miss Blair.' He waved her ahead of him towards a plump, fresh-faced woman standing in the open doorway.

'You will be Miss Blair,' she called, smiling. 'Welcome. I am Jean MacPhail.'

Flora hurried to take her outstretched hand, smiling ruefully. 'How nice to meet you. But as you can see I'm flabbergasted. I wasn't expecting anything remotely as grand!'

Jean MacPhail chuckled as her husband excused himself to drive off on another errand. She led the way through an oak-panelled hall to a small, uncluttered room with a view of the loch from its windows. Flora barely noticed the beautiful old furniture or the walls lined with green watered silk, paled almost to silver in places. All her attention was centred instantly on a collection of exquisite water-colours depicting the loch in varying mood.

Jean went off to fetch a tray of supper for the traveller, leaving Flora alone to come to terms with 'Aunt Jenny's little place in Scotland'. She moved from picture to picture, laughing out loud as she pictured her great-aunt's glee. In the letter left with her will Genista Lyon had explained how she came by the tenancy of Inch Cottage, but made no mention of the size and value of the property. It was suddenly so much more a problem than expected that Flora decided she needed food and sleep before her jaded brain could even begin to wrestle with it.

'You will want to wash your hands,' stated Jean as she backed into the room with a laden tray. 'There's a wee cloakroom across the hall, but be quick or this will cool. Afterwards I'll show you the rest of the house.'

Obediently Flora went to tidy up, admiring old-fashioned mahogany and brass fittings as her stomach gave a very unladylike rumble to remind her that coffee and some British Rail sandwiches had been her only sustenance since leaving home that morning.

'There now.' Jean installed her in a chair near the fire, whipped a snow-white linen napkin across Flora's knees and handed her a bowl of clear tomato soup garnished with a spiral of cream. 'While you eat that I will fetch the rest.'

'This is very kind of you, Mrs MacPhail,' said Flora gratefully. 'I do hope I'm not putting you to too much trouble.'

'None at all—and please call me Jean.' She smiled mischievously. 'I've been wed to Donald for twenty-five years and his mother dead for ten of them, but to me Mrs MacPhail is still my mother-in-law.'

Flora dispatched her soup, and the poached cutlet of salmon which followed, while Jean bustled in and out of the room, taking away dishes and bringing more, and at last consenting to sit down herself when she arrived with a tea-tray.

'It's not coffee you should be drinking at this time of night,' she said firmly as she poured.

'Tea is perfect—I drank too much coffee on the train.' Flora smiled gratefully. 'Thank you so much, Jean. That was a delicious supper.'

The other woman eyed her speculatively over her teacup. 'Miss Lyon never said much about this place, then?'

Flora shook her head. Her great-aunt had been deliberately secretive about her regular trips to Scotland. 'She was always vague about the cottage. My family had the impression she rented it through the kindness of a friend she met on holiday as a girl.'

'True enough,' said Jean drily. 'Did you never know who the friend was, then, Miss Blair?'

'Not a word, until I read the startling letter she left me with the will. None of my family had the slightest inkling of the double life Aunt Jenny led right up to the day she died.' Flora smiled ruefully. 'I adored her. I used to plague her to let me come with her when she escaped up here every summer. But she said this was her own private place, and one day I'd understand why.' Flora gave the other woman a very straight look. 'Now I do understand why, but I imagine there are people up here who might not.'

'I am not one of them,' said Jean MacPhail emphatically. 'It is difficult for Donald, mind. His loyalties have always been divided. But my blood is mixed. My mother was a Londoner— she was Miss Lyon's maid, as you know, brought all the way from England every year. When she married my father it caused quite a stir, but now she's gone it's rare that people remember my English blood. But my allegiance, much as I dote on the young laird, has always been to Miss Lyon. She was very good to me, and a lovely lady,' she added sadly. 'Come, then. You'll be wanting to see the rest of the house.'

Flora, her stamina restored by the meal, followed Jean on a tour which began with a large dining-room where twelve could have dined with ease, then on to a vast formal drawing-room, both rooms ghostly under holland covers, as were five of the bedrooms she was shown upstairs. Jean explained that it had been her habit to keep the entire house under covers when Miss Lyon was not in residence.

'There is the main bathroom,' she said, and opened a door to reveal flowered porcelain, more mahogany and brass, fleecy towels embroidered with oak leaves and sprays of broom. Jean hesitated, her hand on the great china knob of the final door. 'And this was your aunt's room. I thought you would wish to sleep there. The bed is aired and it has its own wee bathroom. You'll like to explore it alone, so I shall be downstairs in the kitchen when you want me, then I must away to my own bed. Donald will be back for me soon.'

Left alone, Flora was conscious of a strong feeling of intrusion as she eyed the closed door of her aunt's room. With some reluctance she turned the heavy, smooth knob at last and opened the door, then stood transfixed, confronted by her second surprise of the day. Unlike the austere charm of the rest of the house, Aunt Jenny's private domain exuded uninhibited, erotic invitation. Swagged and fringed damask curtains matched the pink and gold roses wreathing the pale carpet and the silk cushions heaped on the *chaise-longue*, and every piece of furniture in the room was gilded and carved with a sensuality designed to complement the dominance of the opulent brass bed. The entire room was in such contrast to the stark beauty of the view outdoors that Flora could hardly believe her eyes. Even after reading her great-aunt's letter it was difficult to relate such a flagrant love-nest of a room with someone she'd known only as an eccentric, elderly lady.

Flora closed the door softly behind her, drawn instantly to a framed pencil sketch over the fireplace. Hands behind her back, she studied the face of a man with a shock of hair and imperious, hard features, the eyes depicted with such skill that they seemed alive. So, she thought, eyeing the challenging face, you were the man responsible for Aunt Jenny's retreat to Scotland every year, the lover conveniently possessed of a spare house to tuck her away during the short Highland summer.

Flora went downstairs deep in thought to find Jean MacPhail putting china away in the cupboards of a kitchen large enough to cater for a banquet.

'The bedroom was another wee shock,' Jean said, giving Flora a searching look. 'Did you not know about your aunt and the old laird?'

'Not until I read her letter—which was no preparation for the impact of that bedroom.' Flora smiled ruefully. 'She was in her sixties when I was born. I need time to adjust to her as a girl who fell in love with a man who couldn't marry her.'

'My mother said he would have done if he could.' Jean looked uncomfortable. 'Not that it's for me to discuss such things, of course, but it's common knowledge that the old laird never looked at another woman from the moment he met Miss Lyon. He'd had an eye for the ladies before, they say, his marriage being what it was. But never afterwards.'

Flora smiled. 'I'm pleased to hear it, because from Aunt Jenny's letter he was certainly the one great love of *her* life.'

Jean glanced at the big wood-framed clock on the wall. 'Donald will be back soon. I do hope you'll be all right in this place all alone. I wish we were not away to Perth in the morning, but my Ailsa is expecting her first any moment and I've promised we'll be there.'

'I shall be fine,' Flora assured her. 'I'm sorry I had to come a couple of days earlier than originally arranged, but I need to get away again fairly soon for a holiday in France. I'm only grateful you could spare the time to get this place ready for me.' She held out her hand, smiling. 'I don't intend to stay very long, so if I don't see you again thank you very much for all your help.'

Jean took Flora's hand, giving her an oddly blank, dreamy look. 'Oh, I shall see you again, Miss Blair. No doubt about that.' She collected herself hurriedly as a car drew up outside. 'There's Donald. If you will come with us now to our house you can drive the car back here to keep for your own use while we are away, as arranged. Donald's nephew will take us to the station in the morning.'

Donald MacPhail added his doubts about Flora's stay at Inch Cottage. 'You could sleep at our house if you wished,' he suggested diffidently. 'I fear you'll find the loneliness here daunting.'

She shook her head, smiling. 'I shall relish it, Mr MacPhail. I spend most of my time among teenage girls. The peace here will be a welcome change.'

His wife nodded briskly. 'And what could harm her here, Donald? Now, Miss Blair, when you go home you can leave the key up at the house.'

'Which house?' asked Flora as she went with them to the car.

They both looked at her in surprise.

'*The* house,' repeated Jean patiently. She made a sweeping gesture towards the far shore of the loch. 'Ardlochan, across the water there.'

A short time later Flora was back at Inch Cottage, having made her phone call to her parents, and eager for a long night's sleep in the splendour of her great-aunt's bed.

Flora unpacked a few necessary items, then took a swift bath in the pink and ivory extravagance of her aunt's bathroom, marvelling at mirror-lined walls and gold-plated dolphins which gushed hot water. Too sybaritic for words, she thought, smiling as she dried herself on a huge bath-sheet embroidered with more oak leaves and sprays of broom. She brushed out her hair, wove it loosely into a braid as thick as her wrist, then settled herself against piled pillows to read for a while. But after only a page or two her eyes refused to focus. Leaving the bedside lamp on for company in the large, empty house, she slid down in the bed, asleep almost at once.

She woke with a start at some stage in the night, her heart thumping, wondering what had disturbed her. She switched off the lamp and sat upright, listening, then gasped in fright at the sound of a smothered male curse somewhere downstairs. To her astonishment light showed suddenly below her door, and without giving herself time to think she leapt out of bed, seized a brass candlestick from the mantelpiece and ran from the room, down the stairs, brandishing her weapon like an avenging fury. Flora skidded to an abrupt stop in the parlour doorway, her eyes like saucers at the sight of a preposterously attractive male figure in all the glory of full Highland evening dress: black jacket, silver buttons, sporran, kilt, a dirk tucked into one of the hose, brogues with ankle lacings.

'Dear me,' said Flora, when she'd recovered her powers of speech. 'Bonny Prince Charlie, I assume?'

The glamorous stranger looked utterly appalled. 'I apologise,' he forced out, his face rigid with embarrassment. 'Inch Cottage is always dark at night. I thought someone had broken in.' His eyes, piercingly bright as his silver buttons in his dark, olive-skinned face, looked her up and down, lingering deliberately on the slim bare thighs below her satin nightshirt. 'I am Cameron of Ardlochan. You, I take it, are Miss Lyon's relative.'

'Yes,' said Flora, the coolness of her tone masking intense embarrassment. 'If you'll excuse me I'll get my dressing-gown.'

'Please don't trouble,' he said, preparing to leave. 'It was never my intention to linger.'

'Nevertheless, Mr Cameron, since you *are* here perhaps you'd be good enough to stay for just a moment,' said Flora crisply. 'It will save trouble for both of us tomorrow.' Taking his consent for granted, she went back upstairs to wrap herself in a red cotton dressing-gown. She thrust her feet into espadrilles, tidied her hair, and went downstairs again to find her visitor looking very much at home in front of the fireplace in the parlour, his splendour quite in keeping with the beautiful room.

'Allow me to introduce myself,' she began without preamble. 'My name is Blair. I'm Miss Lyon's great-niece.'

He inclined his head in acknowledgement. 'I gathered as much. Is your aunt not coming this year?'

'No, Mr Cameron. You obviously hadn't heard.' Flora cleared her throat. 'She died last week.'

A gleam lit his eyes for a split-second before he schooled his expression to conventional sympathy.

'I've been away. Otherwise, of course, I would have heard the news from Jean MacPhail. And other sources. Please accept my condolences.'

'Thank you,' said Flora formally. 'Won't you sit down, Mr Cameron?'

He shook his head. 'Thank you, no. It's late. I must go.'

She eyed him challengingly. 'Before you do would you mind telling me how you got in? I thought I'd locked everything up very securely.'

He returned the look with hauteur. 'I used my key.'

'Your key?'

'Miss Lyon was fully aware I retained one for my own use,' he assured her. 'I make a habit of checking on Inch Cottage from time to time, or if Jean MacPhail reports anything amiss. It *is* part of my estate,' he reminded her cuttingly.

Flora, though strongly averse to the thought of a house key in someone else's possession, couldn't drum up enough courage to ask her impressive visitor to hand it over. She held out an envelope. 'My aunt asked me to deliver this to you in person, Mr Cameron.'

He took the letter from her, his black-browed frown forbidding. 'I wonder why Miss Lyon thought it necessary to write to me?'

'No doubt the letter will explain.'

'Quite so.' He gave her a small, formal bow. 'Goodnight, then, Miss Blair. I'll see myself out.' He turned away with a swirl of red and green tartan. In the doorway he paused, frowning. 'May I ask why you felt it necessary to play postman in person?'

She met the hard, cold gaze serenely. 'It was Aunt Jenny's stated wish.'

'How long will you stay?'

'Until I've carried out my great-aunt's instructions—however long that takes.' Flora looked at him quizzically. 'Why, Mr Cameron? Is my presence unwelcome? You disappoint me. My aunt always painted such a glowing picture of Highland hospitality.'

His jaw tightened. 'You must stay as long as you wish, of course. Though I would not have thought a stay alone at Inch Cottage would appeal to someone like yourself. Unless, of course,' he added looking her up and down, 'you are not alone.'

'As it happens I am. Apart from playing postman, as you put it, my aim was a short holiday in peace and privacy.' Flora marched past him into the hall and opened the outer door. 'So far I've had little of either. Goodnight, Mr Cameron.'

'You're aware Inch Cottage lacks a telephone?' he said, ignoring her thrust.

'Of course.' Flora looked past him into the still, starlit darkness. 'My aunt never saw the need for one. Neither shall I.'

'Since you're here for only a *short* time I imagine you won't. Goodnight, then, Miss Blair. My apologies again for the intrusion.' He paused. 'By the way, harking back to your remark about Bonny Prince Charlie, only my grandfather was Charles Edward. My name is James. Am I allowed to ask yours?'

To Flora it suddenly seemed wildly unreal to be standing in the doorway of a strange house on the edge of a loch in the wilds of Scotland, talking to a man who looked as though he'd stepped from one of the portraits in the drawing-room of Inch Cottage. 'Flora,' she said unwillingly.

Her visitor laughed derisively. 'Flora? No wonder you saw me as the ghost of Bonny Prince Charlie!'

'I was named at the request of my great-aunt,' said Flora with dignity. 'And even a Sassenach like me knows that unlike you, Mr Cameron, Charles Edward Stuart had reddish-blond hair. Goodnight.'

CHAPTER TWO

IN BED again, but wide awake, Flora lay simmering with resentment towards the intruder for disturbing her sleep. Cameron of Ardlochan indeed! She'd almost heard the skirl of the pipes as he'd announced himself. Something about the arrogant laird had put her teeth thoroughly on edge, standing there in the parlour as though he owned the place. Which he did, she reminded herself, then smiled wickedly. When he read Aunt Jenny's letter he'd get a nasty shock, just the same. Too bad he'd been so stiff-necked and unfriendly. Before their abrasive little encounter she'd been fully prepared to hand over the tenancy to Inch Cottage and be on her way. Now he could just dangle a while before she let him off the hook.

Flora gave up trying to sleep and switched the light on, deciding to read until she felt drowsy again. But the portrait over the fireplace kept diverting her eye from the page— Charles Edward Cameron, her aunt's Bonny Prince in person. His grandson resembled him hardly at all except for the same damn-your-eyes expression Aunt Jenny's pencil had reproduced so cleverly. And unlike his grandson's coal-black hair it was plain, even from a pencil sketch, that Charles Edward's had been fair like his namesake's. James Cameron's colouring probably came from his French grandmother, thought Flora, remembering Aunt Jenny's letter.

She lay back against the pillows, her eyes dreamy as she thought of the rapture her aunt must have experienced with her lover in this very bed. But now both Genista and her lover were dead and all their passion cold. Or was it? Flora looked about her at the room, finding it all too easy to imagine it haunted by echoes of a love so strong that it had transcended all the social barriers of the day. Abandoning her book, Flora took her aunt's letter from her bag to read again, its contents far more compelling than fiction now she was actually here in the setting for the romance.

The letter was an extraordinary document. It had come as a great shock to both Flora and her parents, since no one in the family had known anything of the story behind Jenny Lyon's cottage in the Highlands. Over the years they'd taken their eccentric relative's annual trips to Scotland for granted, assuming, as she'd meant them to, that her sole reason was the production of the water-colours which fetched such impressive prices in the London art gallery which handled her work.

The letter was written in the copperplate script Aunt Jenny's artist's hand had retained right to the end.

My dearest Flora. When you read this I shall be dead, and unable to see your reaction. Such a pity! Please show it to your parents once you've stopped laughing, darling. *You* come from a different day and age so you'll merely be amused by my deathbed revelations, but I'm afraid Edward and Lucy may find them hard to swallow. Never mind, it's all over, and no harm done. But now the leading players in my little tale are merely ghosts I want you to know exactly why I always travelled to Scotland alone, except for Amy at first. But in time I lost her to the Highlands, too. Not that this was a bad thing at all, as it turned out, though I sadly missed her cooking afterwards during my Bloomsbury winters of discontent.

Flora chuckled to herself in the great brass bed. How she missed Aunt Jenny.

Genista Lyon had been the younger daughter of parents who believed in marriage as the ineluctable destiny for a girl of her background. But when the tragedy of the First World War depleted the ranks of eligible suitors the young Genista persuaded her parents, after much pleading and coaxing, to let her take up the university scholarship she'd won. In due course she graduated with a creditable fine arts degree and gained a teaching post at a very superior girls' boarding-school in the Midlands. There she became fast friends with one Moira Carstairs who taught history. Moira hailed from Inverness, and at the end of that first school year invited Genista to spend part of her summer holiday at the Carstairs home in the capital of the Highlands.

At this point fate, content to allow the competent Genista to get on with her own life up to that point, decided to step in. The first leisurely days of the holiday were taken up with bicycle rides to picturesque locations where Genista could paint to her heart's content while Moira read from Sir Walter Scott and presided over the picnic basket. But one day a heavy shower of rain hastened their return, both girls hastily skewering on hats and donning waterproof capes for the ride back on laden bicycles. Genista was a far better artist than cyclist.

When one of the new, noisy motor cars rounded a corner in her wake she looked over her shoulder in alarm and promptly lost control of her mount, which collapsed, wheels spinning, depositing rider and paintbox in an undignified heap. The shiny car stopped dead, a man leapt out as Moira came bowling back, both of them converging simultaneously on the enraged Genista to come to her aid. Struggling to extricate herself from a tangle of machinery and artist's paraphernalia, Genista was obliged to accept a hard, gloved hand which whisked her to her feet with such force that her hat fell off and her great mass of amber hair fell down her back, showering pins in all directions as the rain came down in torrents and soaked them all. Aunt Jenny wrote:

Looking back on the incident, it was highly amusing—Moira flapping about like a mother hen while this stranger in a dustcoat whipped off his gloves, cap and goggles in the pouring rain and without so much as a by your leave ran his hands all over me for broken bones, as if I were a horse.

During the examination the stranger soon realised that the damsel in distress, far from being a horse, was a very attractive young woman, with flashing dark eyes and a skin flushed with temper. Genista Lyon pushed his hands away, incensed, and told him in no uncertain terms what she thought of idiots who drove nasty, smelly contraptions which threatened innocent people's safety. Charles Edward Cameron apologised with grace and introduced himself, winning a startled glance from Moira as she responded in kind. He offered to drive the ladies home, but Genista flatly refused and pedalled off with Moira through the pouring rain, her laughter floating back to Charles Cameron as he wrenched in vain on the car's starting handle.

Next day two bouquets of flowers arrived at the Carstairs home, with a note of apology for each of the ladies for any distress caused the day before. Moira's family were much put out by the card sent with the flowers. Charles Edward Cameron of Ardlochan was a married man, Genista was informed, and therefore not to be encouraged should he seek further contact.

Fate was undeterred. Having thrown Genista Lyon and Charles Cameron together, it had no intention of letting matters stand. Moira developed a feverish cold after her soaking on the expedition, which meant that Genista, made of sterner stuff, was given permission to sketch on the riverbank near the house, with Effie the housemaid for chaperon.

Charles Cameron was staying at the Palace Hotel, a mere stroll along the riverbank from the point where Genista set up her easel that sunlit, fateful afternoon. Effie wheedled permission to walk a wee step with a young waiter from the hotel, with the result that the absorbed artist was alone when a tall figure in an elegant tweed suit cast a long shadow across her easel.

Flora looked across at the portrait, shaking her head at Charles Edward Cameron. 'What chance did Aunt Jenny have against a handsome devil like you?'

When Moira's cold worsened to influenza Genista Lyon insisted on cutting her holiday short. With regrets the Carstairs family bade her farewell and put her on the train, which she promptly left at the next station down the line where Charles Cameron was waiting with his motor car.

'And thus, Flora,' wrote Miss Lyon, 'began my life of sin.'

Flora clasped her hands behind her head, wondering what alchemy Charles Cameron had possessed to keep her aunt faithful to him, even after his death. His marriage, arranged by his father, had been disastrous. His wife, Honorine, a pious, magnificently dowered French lady, disliked marriage, Ardlochan and the Scottish climate with equal intensity. Within the space of a year she grudgingly presented her husband with the required heir, then firmly locked her bedroom door to him and took to spending longer and longer periods in France. Charles Cameron was left to a life centred on his son and his estate, with, very occasionally, a discreet liaison with some lady willing to comfort him for his lack of connubial bliss.

The day he met Genista Lyon he was thirty-two years old, experienced with women, but had never been in love. Neither had Genista, who was ten years younger; she knew nothing about men, and firmly believed marriage was for other women. She never changed her mind. After her first night in Charles Cameron's arms at Inch Cottage she knew beyond all doubt that marriage with any other man was out of the question.

'Honorine was a deeply devout Catholic, strong as a horse, and unlikely to die in the foreseeable future,' wrote Aunt Jenny, 'so the only course open to me was to become Charles Cameron's mistress.'

Having waited so long to fall in love, Charles Cameron did it with the thoroughness he brought to most pursuits. He made the tenancy of Inch Cottage over to Genista for her lifetime for a peppercorn rent, furnished it exactly to her requirements, and left it empty during the long, lonely months when his love was leading the other half of her double life.

Genista's annual stay at Inch Cottage always lasted precisely six weeks, from the middle of July when the summer term finished to the last day of August when Honorine returned from her summer escape to France. September being the great social period of the Scottish calendar, Cameron of Ardlochan's wife was needed to preserve the fiction of their marriage at the countless functions of the season, including the annual house party at Ardlochan where Honorine was required to preside.

A mere six weeks of his love's company per year, however, soon proved far too little for Cameron of Ardlochan. He took to travelling abroad during the Easter holidays. And so did Genista Lyon. Officially she went to Rome or the Greek Islands with a colleague. But in reality she spent the time with Charles Cameron, and the paintings produced during these idylls were, without exception, views from the first-floor balcony of whatever hotel bedroom they occupied.

Genista Lyon's annual visits to Inch Cottage with attendant English maid—Amy was employed at the school otherwise, and glad to keep Miss Lyon's secret in exchange for a long, free holiday every year—were greeted in time with a strange kind of acceptance by the inhabitants of Ardlochan. The estate was vast, and Inch Cottage a long way from Ardlochan House. And those who served the laird were pleased rather than otherwise that their master had found happiness with the young English lady who spent most of the daylight hours at her easel, painting the surrounding landscape.

Aunt Jenny's letter told the rest of her story.

I have never ceased to miss Charles, which is why I always kept up my annual summer pilgrimage to Inch Cottage these past ten years since he's gone. To the place where we were so happy together. Indulge an eccentric old woman, Flora, by staying there yourself for a while. Charles always insisted that the tenancy was mine to do with as I wished, and until very recently I fully intended it to revert automatically to the estate and young James. But lately I've become convinced that you must see it first.

I hope you will indulge a sentimental old woman, Flora, for you have always been the child I could never allow myself to bear to Charles. I chose your name, and it has always been a great joy to me that you followed in the more respectable of my footsteps. So humour me this one last time and spend a few days at Inch Cottage. My solicitor assures me I may hand on the tenancy to you if I wish. You, I know, will do what's right, Flora.

Flora looked about her at the frankly erotic room, wondering just exactly what her great-aunt thought of as 'right'. Her own original plan had been a short stay at Inch Cottage before handing the tenancy back to the present laird. Her eyes danced as they met the pencilled gaze in the drawing.

'That's what you expected, too, I suppose,' she told Charles Cameron out loud. 'You thought Aunt Jenny would meekly hand the cottage back to your grandson when the time came. So did *he*! The present Cameron of Ardlochan was very put out to find Miss Lyon's "relative" in possession, which, whether he likes it or not, is perfectly lawful. I checked.'

Flora woke early next morning to pearly light and a stiff breeze in the trees sheltering Inch Cottage. Yawning, she stumbled from bed to dress in jeans and jersey, thick socks and rubber-soled deck shoes. While the kettle boiled in the immaculate kitchen she went outside to snip a sprig of the bright gold broom and put it in a tumbler on the broad window-sill, smiling gleefully at the bright splash of colour as she made toast to eat with some of Jean MacPhail's marmalade.

After breakfast she went outside to explore. The pearl-grey of earlier had given way to a warmer, brighter light, investing the loch with an allure which almost changed her mind, tempting her to try her hand at capturing it.

'First you walk,' she told herself firmly.

Flora locked the door and made for the loch. The air was cool and soft against her skin as she kept to the shore path, which led her round headlands, over the crests of others, in and out of woodland, her feet crunching on shingle as in places she scrambled past boulders at the water's edge. The loch gleamed aquamarine-pale in the early sunlight, in a setting of such rugged grandeur that Flora found it all too easy to understand Genista Lyon's love for her Highland retreat.

After walking for half an hour or so Flora sat down on a boulder for a breather, her eyes on a stark stone tower which reared up from a headland across the water like a jagged tooth. A shaft of sunlight struck through breaches in its walls, confirming that the ruin was definitely not Ardlochan, but very moody and romantic at a distance just the same. Wishing she'd brought her sketchbook, Flora resumed her walk, and eventually caught sight of a house across the loch. It was imposing, set back from a small beach and shielded by a stand of Scottish pine. Even from a distance she could see it was a grand relation of Inch Cottage, except that it was much larger, and had conical towers at either end. If it had been French it could have been described as a château, and that it was Ardlochan Flora had no doubt at all.

She was disappointed. Somehow she'd expected James Cameron's home to be more like the ruined tower, a dour stronghold defended with its owners' blood in times gone by.

After her long ramble Flora was pleasantly tired by the time she reached the path which led through the woods to Inch Cottage, but her feeling of well-being evaporated abruptly when she saw a mud-splashed Land Rover waiting outside the house. A tall, familiar figure was pacing beside it, and even from a distance it was obvious that Cameron of Ardlochan was awaiting her return with ill-concealed impatience.

Flora deliberately made no effort to hurry. When she was within earshot she smiled coolly and wished her hostile landlord a polite good-morning.

'Good morning, Miss Blair.' He made no attempt to return her smile, his eyes arctic as he gestured towards the house. 'May I come in for a moment? I'd like a word if you can spare the time.'

'Of course.' Flora glanced over her shoulder at him as she fitted her key in the lock. 'I'm surprised you didn't let yourself in to wait for me in comfort.'

James Cameron followed her through the hall into the kitchen, looking even more formidable in a jersey and old corduroys than in his romantic regalia of the night before. He raised a hostile eyebrow.

'Certainly not. Last night was a mistake, Miss Blair. You need fear no more intrusions on my part.'

'Oh, good,' said Flora lightly. 'Nice to know I can rest easy in my aunt's bed. May I offer you some coffee?'

He shook his head brusquely. 'Thank you, no. This is not a social visit.'

'No,' she agreed, and perched on a corner of the kitchen table. 'I don't suppose it is. So what can I do for you, Mr Cameron?'

'I demand to know your intentions regarding Inch Cottage.'

Flora looked at him levelly, secretly quite put out. Such unfriendly reaction from the opposite sex was something new in her experience. And James Cameron's loss. Face to face with the cold enmity in his eyes her resolve hardened. If he'd shown her the slightest civility she'd have handed over the tenancy to him then and there and gone off to France without another thought. But, confronted with a man who saw her as nothing but an obstacle to his inheritance, Flora had no compunction about keeping to the plan she'd made in the wakeful hours after his departure the night before.

'I visited a solicitor before I came,' she informed him. 'He, in turn, consulted with an Edinburgh advocate to make sure he was perfectly clear about Scottish law on the subject.'

James Cameron's brows met like a black bar across his prominent nose. 'What the hell are you saying?'

Flora slid off the table, flicking her braid over her shoulder. She walked over to the window-sill, took the sprig of broom from its jar and turned to face him.

'I gather the only rent your grandfather ever demanded from my great-aunt was what you call a feu duty in this part of the world—a right to the use of the land, or in this case of Inch Cottage, for a fixed annual payment.' She held out the sprig of broom, her dark eyes as cold as his. 'In their case the payment was an annual fee of a sprig of broom, or, to call it by its botanical name, genista—a play on my great-aunt's name. My solicitor tells me that because she handed down the tenancy to me I am quite within my rights to remain at Inch Cottage for as long as I care to pay the agreed annual feu duty to the present landlord.'

James Cameron stared down at the yellow sprig in her hand, then up at her face, his eyes like chips of ice. 'Are you saying you mean to go through with this nonsense?'

'Indeed I am,' she said gently. 'And there's no nonsense about it. Feu duties are a touch archaic these days, but I'm assured I'm not breaking any law.' She tossed the broom down on the table like a gauntlet. 'There's your rent, Mr Cameron.'

Even on such short acquaintance Flora could tell James Cameron was the type of man rarely at a loss for words, however laconic. But for the moment he was quite obviously speechless. Flora resumed her perch on the corner of the table, one foot swinging nonchalantly as she waited for him to speak.

'I suppose,' he said bitterly at last, 'I should have expected this after reading Miss Lyon's letter.'

'Did it tell you what she had in mind?'

'She wrote that she was handing the tenancy over to her great-niece with the conviction that her dearest Flora would do what she herself would have wished.' He laughed mirthlessly. 'No doubt Miss Lyon was more precise in her letter to you, Miss Blair.'

'Not in so many words.' Flora shrugged. 'She told me your grandfather probably expected her to hand the place back when she'd finished with it. But for some reason she decided to pass the tenancy over to me, which, I am informed, was completely within her power to do.'

'In that case,' he said grimly, 'there's no more to be said. Thank you for sparing me your time, Miss Blair.'

'I'll see you to the door,' she said promptly, sliding from the table.

'Please don't trouble. I shan't trespass on your time or your property any longer than necessary.' His eyes met hers for a long moment, bright and clear as glass. 'Perhaps after you've been here for a while, when the lochan is in less welcoming mood, you may change your mind about staying at Inch Cottage. Because I trust your solicitor made it clear that *staying* here is all you can do. Inch Cottage still belongs to me. You are not entitled to sell it, nor to let it out to paying guests.'

'What a shame,' said Flora flippantly. 'And there was I thinking I'd come in for a nice little earner!' She strolled ahead of him to the front door and opened it wide. 'Don't worry, Mr Cameron. All I have in mind is a nice rest away from it all—now and then.'

He eyed her narrowly. 'So your mind is made up.'

'Yes. For the time being, anyway.' She smiled at him sweetly. 'And, just to pre-empt any other edicts from the laird, I'm aware that my tenancy doesn't allow me to remove anything from the house. So while you're here perhaps you'd like to take an inventory to make sure I don't run off with the silver at the end of my stay.'

'I'm glad you find this all so amusing,' he said tightly.

Her chin lifted. 'I don't find it amusing in the least. Frankly, Mr Cameron, I find your attitude deeply offensive.'

James Cameron's face darkened. 'If it is I feel justified, Miss Blair. I was resigned to the fact that Inch Cottage remained at Miss Lyon's disposal during her lifetime, but I strongly resent the fact that on some whim she's willed the tenancy to a stranger.'

'Hardly a stranger!'

'You are to me, Miss Blair. I'll bid you good morning.' And without further ado James Cameron sprang up into the Land Rover and drove off down the track through the woods at breakneck speed.

Flora watched him out of sight, then turned to look up at Inch Cottage, which suddenly seemed less like a love-nest than a bone of contention.

CHAPTER THREE

WITH only a transistor radio for company indoors, Flora was grateful for fine weather which allowed her to get out of the house each day. Sketchbook at the ready, she set out to explore on foot, but never got very far before settling down on a fallen log or a boulder to draw views already familiar to her from Aunt Jenny's work. Her own style, harsher and less pictorial, targeted the transience underlying the serenity of the loch, a threatening undertone to her drawings very much in keeping with her general mood after her run-in with the hostile laird of Ardlochan.

But as her eyes and hands collaborated in producing some of the best work she'd ever done Flora's conscience pricked her about laying even temporary claim to Inch Cottage. She had no earthly right to it, she knew perfectly well. And, unknown to the autocratic laird, she had no intention of lingering there a second longer than the few days requested by her great-aunt. James Cameron's attitude was to blame, she told herself irritably. He'd roused some inner devil which egged her on to make him suffer for a while before she let him have his precious property back.

After a day or two of her own company, Flora decided to drive further afield in the MacPhails' car, and spent a pleasant afternoon in Fort William exploring the museum and the shops, buying new-baked bread and fresh vegetables and fish to supplement the supplies left her by Jean. But on the journey home the weather took a turn for the worse. Rain came down with sudden fury, lashing against the windscreen. The journey seemed twice as long on the way back, partly because Flora was obliged to keep peering for signs to Ardlochan through gloom so absolute that it looked more like nightfall than late afternoon.

Deeply thankful to arrive at Inch Cottage at last, Flora gathered up her packages and fled into the house. She banged the door shut behind her, dumping her shopping on the floor in her eagerness to turn on lights to mitigate the gloom and sudden, overwhelming feeling of loneliness. She scoffed at herself as she put the food away in the kitchen, scornful about fair-weather visitors who chickened out at the first few drops of rain. Only it wasn't just a few drops of rain, but a dark, torrential downpour, which blotted the lochan from sight, and reduced the world outside to a dripping grey wilderness very different from the sunlit paradise of the past few days.

For the first time since her arrival Flora missed her television set. She switched on her radio quickly, needing voices and music in the silent, empty house as she began to cook herself a more elaborate meal than she'd bothered with of late. But grilling fish and cooking vegetables took only so much time, and even after spinning out the meal as long as possible there was still a large slice of the evening left before Flora felt she could decently go to bed.

James Cameron's warning about the loch in stormy mood returned to plague her. No doubt he was sitting across the water in his elegant house, laughing at her at this very moment, certain that Inch Cottage and its isolation would quickly pall now the weather had changed so dramatically. He would soon realise his mistake. She would stick it out to the bitter end even if Charles Edward Cameron's ghost came to haunt her in person—— Which was such a disturbing thought that she dismissed it hurriedly, and took her coffee into the parlour to drink at her leisure, along with a pile of paperback novels and her radio for company.

But for once the written word failed to absorb. Restless and on edge, Flora wandered upstairs to switch on lights for company, then stood at the bedroom window to look out, but there was nothing visible through the curtain of driving rain. Normally she could see the friendly pin-point lights across the water. Tonight she could have been on the moon for all the evidence of other human habitation.

Suddenly Flora's heart leapt as she saw the flash of car headlights, heading towards the house through the rain. Ready to welcome company of any kind, she ran from the room and down the stairs, but before she reached the door the car drove off again. Her disappointment was so intense that she took a moment or two to notice the letter lying on the floor. To her amazement the envelope contained a card engraved with the address of Ardlochan House. Mrs Isobel Cameron requested the pleasure of Miss Blair's company at a small, informal dinner party the following Saturday.

Flora sat down on the settle rather suddenly, staring at the invitation with suspicion. Asked to break bread with the enemy? She tapped a fingernail against her teeth, wondering if James Cameron's wife had some idea of regaining Inch Cottage by more subtle methods than her husband's militant tactics. Flora's eyes narrowed. Saturday was only three days away, which was pretty short notice. But James Cameron knew perfectly well she was alone here. No doubt he was confident that the stranger would not only be eager, but honoured to dine at Ardlochan. And in one way he was right. Flora eyed the gloom outside with a grin. An invitation from the devil himself would be welcome in weather like this.

But to her delight Flora woke next morning to a world washed clean of every cloud. The loch sparkled under a cloudless sky, the sun glinted gold on the broom in the wet green woods, and suddenly Flora couldn't get breakfast over quickly enough in her hurry to explore the newly laundered Eden outside. To make her day complete the postman brought her a letter from home, and waited cheerfully, enjoying a cup of coffee, while she wrote a short note of acceptance to Isobel Cameron.

As soon as Archie Lennox went on his way Flora set out with her sketching materials to capture the ruined tower in less forbidding mood than her two previous studies. Something about the stark stone pile exerted such a pull that she'd decided to feature it in a series of drawings for her bedroom wall at home, as a reminder of her stay at Ardlochan.

Choosing a spot which gave her a different angle on the tower, Flora began to draw with quick, bold strokes, her concentration intense as she worked.

'You're talented,' said a familiar voice in her ear, startling her badly. Flora spun round to find James Cameron looking over her shoulder.

She almost asked him what the blazes he was doing, creeping up on her and scaring her rigid. But with the invitation still fresh in her mind she forced a far from civil good morning.

'You startled me,' she said shortly. 'I didn't hear a car.'

He waved a hand towards the road in the distance. 'I caught sight of you as I was passing, so I parked the Land Rover behind those trees over there.'

Flora closed her sketchbook with a snap and stood up, all her hackles erect at the sight of her unfriendly landlord. This morning he was in better control of his hostility, she noted, but the piercingly bright eyes were as wintry as ever.

'Is there a problem—am I trespassing, Mr Cameron?'

He shook his head. 'Your tenancy of Inch Cottage gives you licence to paint where you please in the neighbourhood. Within reason,' he added deliberately.

'Then why did you stop to talk to me?' she asked, her eyes as cold as his.

He shrugged. 'I was curious to know whether you intend to accept our dinner invitation.'

Flora busied herself with packing her rucksack. 'As it happens, Mr Cameron, I was able to send a note by the postman.'

He waited, his face darkening when she took a perverse pleasure in making him wait for his answer. 'And did you accept?' he was forced to ask.

'Yes, I did. In the end.'

'By which I take it you had doubts.'

Flora's eyes flashed. 'Of course I had doubts! The last thing I expected was hospitality from you in the circumstances, Mr Cameron.'

He raised an eyebrow. 'I suppose I took a certain remark of yours to heart. You were rather scathing about Highland hospitality at our first meeting, if you remember.'

She looked at him levelly. 'How could I forget?'

'So now it's established why the invitation was issued,' he went on conversationally, 'but not why it was accepted.'

'Boredom,' said Flora baldly. 'You were quite right. The charms of Ardlochan tend to pall when obscured by rain. A Saturday night spent at your dinner table won hands down as an alternative to one spent alone at Inch Cottage with only a radio and a pile of books for company.'

His mouth turned down at the corners. 'Are you always as blunt, Miss Blair?'

'Invariably. Why? Do you consider bluntness your own particular prerogative, Mr Cameron?'

James Cameron's mouth tightened, then slowly relaxed as he gave Flora a faint, superior smile. 'Perhaps we should declare a truce until after your visit to Ardlochan House, Miss Blair, since you've done us the honour of gracing our table for an evening.' The slight emphasis he placed on the word 'gracing' brought quick colour to Flora's cheeks.

'Very well,' she said stiffly, inwardly ashamed of her lack of manners. 'Actually I really do appreciate your invitation. I'm surprised you even thought of me as a dinner guest—all things considered.'

Enviably thick lashes descended swiftly to hide a sudden gleam in his eyes. 'At the risk of emulating your bluntness, Miss Blair, I'm not entirely devoid of surprise on the subject myself. May I offer you a lift back?' he added, rather taking the wind out of her sails.

She shook her head, annoyed to find herself slightly flustered. 'It's such a lovely day I'd rather walk, thanks just the same. It's partly why I'm here, after all—fresh air and exercise. And limitless opportunities for sketching, just as Aunt Jenny promised.'

On the point of turning away James Cameron halted in his tracks. 'By the way, were you aware that Miss Lyon left me the water-colours in the parlour at Inch Cottage?'

Flora's eyes flickered. 'All twelve?'

'Yes. But if you'd like one,' he added instantly, 'please feel free to choose whichever you want.'

Her chin lifted. 'Thank you, no. I already own some of Aunt Jenny's work. Besides, it would devalue the set to break it up.'

His smile was faintly patronising. 'I wouldn't have thought so. They're quite charming, of course—and it was very kind of her to leave me anything at all.'

'Have you had them valued?'

'No.' His eyes narrowed. 'Do you think I should?'

'That's up to you.' Flora smiled politely and hoisted her bag. 'Time I was on my way.'

He nodded formally. 'Until Saturday, then. Would you like me to fetch you?'

'No! I mean, no, thanks,' said Flora hurriedly. 'The MacPhails kindly gave me the use of their car.'

James Cameron supplied directions to Ardlochan House, favoured her with the formal nod again, and drove off, leaving Flora to wander back, deep in speculation about the motive behind the dinner invitation. Inch Cottage was at the bottom of it, of course. Mrs Cameron had probably pointed out to her belligerent spouse that honey caught more flies than vinegar. Whatever the reason, it would be entertaining to find out.

The prospect of an evening at Ardlochan House added a certain piquancy to life next day as Flora spent a morning sketching, then drove into Fort William in the afternoon to treat herself to a meal and a trip to the cinema. Saturday dawned so grey and chilly that she spent the morning over her hair, which, like her artistic leanings, had been inherited from Aunt Jenny. Often she was tempted to have it cut, but, secretly convinced it was her only striking feature, she left it long, endured the regular ordeal of drying it, and in general kept it out of the way in a braid which she let hang loose at home, and coiled in a knot when she was teaching. But a dinner party at Ardlochan House seemed to call for something different, which resulted in a morning spent on her crowning glory, trying it out in various ways while she mulled over what was likely to be suitable garb for dinner with a laird.

Flora had originally planned to spend most of the summer vacation in the Perigord region of France, sharing a farmhouse with several friends of both sexes. Genista Lyon's posthumous request had changed things slightly. After discussion with her parents, and a hurried consultation with Tom Harvey, her current escort, who was joining her for the last three weeks in the Perigord, she'd decided to visit Inch Cottage first, taking all the luggage necessary for France along with her so she could travel there direct when she left Ardlochan.

And a very good thing she had, thought Flora, as she took out a dress intended for French socialising, otherwise she'd have had nothing suitable to wear. She eyed her reflection closely as she held the dress against herself in front of Aunt Jenny's baroque gilded mirror. Fluid silk jersey, the colour of milk chocolate, clung in some places and draped seductively in others. She nodded, satisfied. Feminine, but understated—exactly the type of armour necessary for the occasion.

Flora felt quite pleased with her reflection when she checked it in the hall mirror on her way out that evening. Her eyes, lightly accented for the occasion, shone darkly in a face glowing from so much time spent out of doors, their gleam accentuated by her dramatic amber and silver earrings. To show off the latter she'd brushed her hair back, securing it behind her ears then letting the rest hang loose in glossy abundance. As she drove along the road which hugged the loch, Flora felt rather like Cinderella on her way to the ball. Such a pity the prince was married already.

Ardlochan House was even more imposing at close quarters than seen from across the water. Flora turned the car through open gates into a driveway which wound through a belt of woodland to the house standing grey and white and solid below the rising slopes of the glen.

Flora's eyebrows rose as she saw several cars there before her, and rather grand ones at that. This really was a dinner party, then—not just a bribery-motivated gesture by the Camerons. Or perhaps one of their guests had dropped out at the last minute, and the real reason for Flora Blair's invitation was to make up a number. She squared her shoulders, her slender heels crunching on gravel as she made her way past colourful borders and closely cut lawns to the main door of the house. She frowned, puzzled, wondering why James Cameron needed Inch Cottage so badly when he had a place like this to live in. Then she braced herself as the man himself emerged from the house to greet her.

James Cameron as host, it was obvious at first glance, was a different proposition from James Cameron the hostile landlord. For a start he was smiling warmly, which transformed his face to a quite astonishing degree as he held out his hand in greeting. 'Welcome, Miss Blair.'

Flora, wary of this new, smiling James Cameron, took the hand briefly. 'Good evening. I'm disappointed.'

One of his black eyebrows rose. 'With the house?'

'No.' She waved a hand at his impeccable dark suit. 'I was expecting a glamorous kilt.'

His eyes travelled slowly from the tips of her shoes to her hair, where they lingered in rather unsettling appreciation. 'While no one, Miss Blair, could be disappointed with *your* appearance. Would it be rude to ask what you've done to your hair?'

'No. And I haven't done anything much. It just looks different when it's loose.'

'An understatement!'

His tone won him a narrowed look from his guest as she preceded him into a stone-flagged hall with a massive fireplace surmounted by the type of shield Flora had seen in the museum—a circular targe mounted like a central sun with rays formed by basket-hilted swords. Voices and laughter issued from an open doorway leading off the hall, sending a slight *frisson* of nerves down her spine as her host ushered her into a room full of animated people. Silence fell, all heads swivelling as one as he led Flora towards a handsome woman with greying dark hair.

'Mother,' said James Cameron, 'this is Miss Flora Blair.'

The woman smiled cordially. 'Good evening—welcome to Ardlochan. I am Isobel Cameron. So good of you to come at such short notice.'

Isobel Cameron was James's *mother*? Flora's polite smile masked surprise, coupled with another reaction she had no time to examine. 'Not at all. It was very kind of you to ask me.'

Searching dark eyes met Flora's for a moment.

'We pride ourselves on our hospitality in this part of the world, Miss Blair,' said Mrs Cameron after a pause. 'Come and meet everyone, my dear.' She took Flora on a brisk tour of the other guests: the Urquharts, who were old family friends, a suave legal gentleman by the name of Drummond with his pretty, friendly wife, and a younger couple introduced as the son and daughter of the Urquharts.

'Ewen, Catriona and James all ran wild together as children,' said Mrs Cameron.

'We still do on occasion,' said Ewen Urquhart, grinning as he shook Flora's hand.

'Are you here on holiday, Miss Blair?' His sister smiled, cold and confident in jade silk which clung lovingly to every curve before it stopped short halfway down rounded, tanned thighs. Unlike her sandy-haired brother, Catriona Urquhart was very dark, with short black hair slicked behind her ears to show emerald drops which rivalled the glitter in her eyes as she took in every detail of Flora's appearance.

Daddy must be loaded, thought Flora. And I thought my dress clung too much! I look like a nun compared with this lady. 'Not exactly,' she said aloud, shaking her head in polite refusal to the champagne a maid was offering.

Provided with fruit punch instead, and delicious morsels of toast spread with salmon flaked in cream, Flora set out to enjoy herself. One look at Catriona was enough to see that James's sexy childhood playmate regarded him as her own particular property. There was a definite 'hands off' in her attitude to Flora, who decided gleefully that the evening held definite promise of entertainment.

The drawing-room was furnished with a pleasing *mélange* of heavy Jacobean furniture, delicate French pieces and comfortable modern sofas. Oil-paintings in gilded frames were everywhere, one of them a portrait of an imperious youth with long fair curls who could only have been Charles Edward Stuart, the Young Pretender himself. When the company moved to the dining-room Flora found it even more attractive. Sheraton sideboards lived in harmony with Windsor chairs and a vast mahogany table set with Limoges porcelain and thistle-shaped goblets. But it was the centre-piece of glossy green leaves and sprigs of broom on a shallow silver dish which caught Flora's attention.

She looked up to meet a significant gleam in James Cameron's eye as he took his place at the head of the table.

'Agnes, our treasure, is good with flowers,' he said, straight-faced.

'What an unusual idea to use broom!' remarked Anna Drummond.

'I have a weakness for it,' said James, looking directly into Flora's eyes.

As a dinner partner he was attentive, almost too attentive from Flora's point of view. She had difficulty in relating to this new, charming James Cameron. It gave her respite when he turned to Anna Drummond from time to time, and talked to others round the table, leaving Flora to the attention of Ewen Urquhart, who made it very plain he was delighted with the arrangement.

'What brings you to this part of the world, Miss Blair?' he asked, as they began on the cock-a-leekie served for the soup course.

'A form of pilgrimage,' said Flora, aware that every ear at the table was strained to hear. 'I came to the Highlands for peace and quiet. So far, however, I find life here remarkably lively.'

James Cameron raised a wry eyebrow in her direction, then embarked on a humorous, if edited account of their first meeting to the table at large. The laughter which greeted his story was kindly enough in general, but Catriona arrowed a malicious glance down the table.

'Goodness, Miss Blair, *what* a surprise to find a man in your room in the middle of the night.'

Flora's hackles rose. She smiled sweetly. 'A fright rather than a surprise—though to be accurate it wasn't actually my bedroom. I had to pluck up courage to go downstairs to face my intruder. It was *then* I had the surprise. I thought Bonny Prince Charlie had come over the sea from Skye to haunt me.'

'But I'm told, on the best authority, that *he* had fair hair,' murmured James under cover of general laughter, while Isobel Cameron patiently explained to Mrs Urquhart that James had been driving home from a formal dinner by the way of the loch road, when he decided to investigate a light in a house that should have been dark.

'But where was that, James?' demanded Catriona. 'Surely the only place you pass that way is Inch Cottage.'

'That's right,' said Flora serenely, laying down her spoon. 'I'm the new tenant.'

Everyone bar the Camerons and Hamish Drummond, the advocate in charge of Ardlochan's legal affairs, stared at her in astonishment.

'I thought that place was kept solely for old Miss Lyon's use,' said Mrs Urquhart.

'Miss Lyon died recently,' James informed her.

'But surely it was supposed to revert to you when the old girl finally snuffed it,' said Ewen in surprise.

'Miss Lyon was my great-aunt,' said Flora, before James could speak. 'She passed the tenancy of Inch Cottage on to me.'

Isobel Cameron quickly put an end to the ensuing pause by introducing a new topic of con-

versation as the soup-plates were cleared. Ewen
cast an uneasy look at James before apologising in an undertone to Flora.

'I'm very sorry, Miss Blair. I'm famous for
putting my foot in it, but I meant no offence,
I swear.'

'I'm not offended,' she assured him, un-
ruffled. 'You merely voiced everyone else's
thoughts.'

Confronted with venison collops, Flora
realised she should have eaten only a mouthful
of soup to have any hope of coping with the
main course.

'You don't care for venison?' asked James.

'I've never eaten it before,' she confessed.
'It's delicious, but I'm used to a one-course
supper at Inch Cottage. Will I incur your wrath
if I don't clear my plate?'

'If you smile at me like that,' he said, so
quietly that no one else could hear, 'whatever
else you may incur, it won't be my wrath.'

Flora stared at him, unable to believe her
ears, then turned away hastily, finding it difficult to concentrate on Ewen Urquhart's banter
for some time. Could the laird actually be
flirting with her? If so, she had a very good
idea why!

'Are you not drinking any wine?' asked Ewen later, in a patient tone which indicated that he'd asked the question once already.

Flora gave him a dazzling smile by way of compensation. 'No, I'm not. I'm afraid I'm one of those barbarians who actively dislike it.'

'Pity. This is damned good burgundy, James.'

'My father laid it down. Not much of it left now, more's the pity.' James invited Flora to try a creamy smoked cheese produced locally. 'I'm very fond of this. I think you'll like it.'

Flora, who was equally fond of cheese, refused regretfully, her appetite depressed by the constant scrutiny of green eyes further down the table. Catriona Urquhart, more interested in James's dinner partner than either of her own, was patently bent on making the newcomer uncomfortable, a feeling reinforced when the ladies left the men at table to go upstairs.

Catriona took it upon herself to escort Flora to a vast bedroom which, even at this time of year, had an atmosphere of such unrelenting chill that Flora hurried over repairs to her face and hair.

'Are you from London?' asked Catriona, perched on the carved four-poster bed.

'Gloucestershire, actually.'

'What do you do for a living?'

'I teach art in a girls' school.'

Catriona's eyes narrowed. 'Really! Following in Miss Lyon's footsteps, then. Isn't that what *she* did when she was young? Until she became mistress to the old laird, I mean. Really hit the jackpot then, of course.'

Flora's eyes glinted coldly. 'My great-aunt was a teacher, yes. Later she made a living from her paintings.'

'Do your ambitions lie in that direction, too?' drawled Catriona, then her face hardened. 'If so make sure that's *all* you have in mind. If you've any fancy ideas about history repeating itself, forget it. *James* doesn't need a mistress—take it from me!'

Making no attempt to hide her distaste, Flora ran a comb through her hair then picked up her bag. 'There. Now, Miss Urquhart, would you be kind enough to direct me to a bathroom before we join the others?'

After she'd made her way back to the drawing-room alone Flora was grateful to find Isobel Cameron beckoning her to a place beside her on a sofa. She engaged Flora in a friendly discussion on the local countryside until the men returned, when Ewen Urquhart promptly drew up a chair alongside Flora. Catriona, circulating smugly with coffee-cups to let Flora know she was an intimate at Ardlochan, looked daggers at James as he perched himself on the arm of the sofa alongside Flora to offer her a drink.

'You've been abstemious all evening. Can I not persuade you to some cognac, or port?' He smiled challengingly as Anna Drummond engaged Ewen in conversation. 'Or would you like a wee dram?'

Flora nodded matter-of-factly. 'Yes, I would. As long as it *is* wee. Single malt—Glenlivet if you have it, please.'

His eyes gleamed with amusement. 'I do indeed. You're a surprising lady.'

'It's the only drink I care for. And only then on special occasions.'

A quizzical black eyebrow rose. 'And this is a special occasion, Flora?'

'Why, yes. It's my first social occasion in Scotland—James.' Still angry from her run-in with Catriona, who was eyeing them resentfully, Flora gave James a brilliant smile, then turned away to talk to Anna Drummond and Ewen, finding their genuine friendliness balm to her soul after Catriona's declaration of war.

Shortly before midnight Flora began to flag, finding an evening among total strangers surprisingly draining after her days of solitude. When she felt she'd stayed long enough for good manners she rose to make her goodbyes all round and thanked her hostess for a delightful evening.

'Not at all,' said Isobel Cameron warmly. 'You must come again. It is rare we are privileged to entertain visitors from the south at Ardlochan. You must find it lonely at Inch Cottage.'

Flora shook her head. 'Restful rather than lonely, Mrs Cameron. I've been fortunate with the weather. I spend most of my time when it's fine sketching this spectacular scenery of yours.'

'Just like your great-aunt.' Isobel Cameron smiled. 'You must come to tea soon, my dear.'

'Why, thank you,' said Flora, touched. 'I'd like that very much.'

'How did you enjoy your first taste of Highland hospitality?' asked James as he walked with her to the car.

Flora gave him a wry smile. 'I felt it had a touch of Culloden about it—only this time you lot won, hands down!'

'I think honours were pretty even, myself, Flora Blair.' He paused, looked down at her, his eyes unreadable in the gloom. 'And I'd rather you didn't think of me as the enemy.'

She eyed him suspiciously. 'Why?'

His teeth gleamed white in the darkness of his face. 'I would have thought that was ob-

CHAPTER FOUR

WHEN Flora woke next morning, she was surprised by a fancy to prolong her stay at Inch Cottage. For one thing Catriona Urquhart's warning was a challenge she couldn't resist, and for another she found James Cameron's indications of thaw highly intriguing. It would be very interesting indeed to learn how he meant to persuade her into giving up the tenancy. There would be lots of summer left to spend in France. Her share of the holiday costs had already been paid, and in any case she'd still arrive long before Tom was due to join her. She smiled, stretching luxuriously in the great brass bed. For the time being Ardlochan held rather more interest than the Perigord, not least because of the laird's thought-provoking reference to siege.

The arrival of the jealous Catriona the night before had put an end to conversation, and James's parting from his guest had of necessity been formal. So now, thought Flora, the next move was up to him. If he intended to make one.

The morning was dismal and wet, and Flora was making her second pot of coffee of the day when she heard a loud knock on the front door and opened it to find James Cameron on her doorstep, brandishing a polythene bag.

'Good morning. I've brought you a present.'

Flora blinked. 'Why, good morning—won't you come in?'

'Thank you.' He followed her into the hall, tall and rather overpowering in a caped, full-length waxed raincoat, an ancient tweed hat pulled low over his eyes. He removed the latter, and stood looking down at her in a manner intended, she suspected, to unsettle her.

'Would you care for some coffee?' she asked.

'I would, very much.' James followed her to the kitchen, divesting himself of his raincoat as he handed her the polythene bag. To Flora's delight it contained several Sunday papers.

'I collected them with ours,' he explained, sitting at the table. 'In this weather it seemed unlikely you'd fancy driving for them yourself.'

'That's extraordinarily kind of you,' said Flora, filling coffee-cups. She looked up at him very directly. 'Not to mention unexpected.'

He returned the look steadily. 'I can't pretend it was my idea. It was my mother's. Which brings me to the main reason for my visit. She wondered if you'd care to come to tea this afternoon.'

Flora felt taken aback. 'How—how very kind of her.'

'Mother realises it's a bit soon, but she'd forgotten she's off to Edinburgh tomorrow, to stay with friends. She thought you might not be here when she got back. The tea party is entirely her own idea, I assure you.'

'Unlike the dinner invitation?'

'That was mine.'

Flora regarded him speculatively. 'And I'm still wondering why.'

James shrugged. 'I've told you why. It's quite simple. Your remark about Highland hospitality rankled. But from my mother's point of view it was no big deal to invite a charming young woman to grace her dinner table!'

Flora looked sceptical. 'Even though she's frustrating your plans for Inch Cottage?'

He eyed her down his prominent Highland nose. 'Perhaps it's all part of a softening-up process to gain my ends.'

'The thought had occurred to me.'

'I shan't try to turn you out in the snow, I promise.'

'Legally you're not able to,' Flora reminded him. 'But please tell your mother I'll be happy to take tea with her this afternoon.' She smiled. 'I took it for granted the dinner invitation was from your wife, you know.'

A dark eyebrow arched satirically. 'Had no one seen fit to inform you of my single state?'

She shook her head. 'The MacPhails refrained from discussing you at all, and I've talked to no one else, barring the postman.'

'It must have set your mind at rest to know the truth.'

Her eyes narrowed. 'Why?'

'If I'd been married you might have had qualms about history repeating itself.'

Flora's mouth tightened. 'If you mean Aunt Jenny and your grandfather, how could it? Even in the unlikely event of you or me being inclined that way, life is very different these days. The only kind of mistress I'm cut out to be, Mr Cameron, is the educational variety.'

'Pity.' He looked at her analytically for a moment, then turned his attention to the large, cheerful kitchen. 'You know, I hardly ever set foot in here until recently. I was very jealous of Miss Lyon when I was a boy. She was only here for a short time every year, but her visits always coincided with my school holiday, and when she was around my grandfather had no time for anyone else, not even me. I suppose because my father died when I was young I was much closer to my grandfather than most boys of my age. He was a wonderful old character.'

'He must have been,' agreed Flora, refilling their cups. 'Aunt Jenny was a strong character herself, yet from the moment she met Charles Cameron she never looked at another man.'

'But she can't have done too badly from their association,' said James bluntly. 'Since she lived in London after she retired I assume the means were supplied by my grandfather.'

Flora glared at him. 'Certainly not! Her income was supplied by her paintbrush. Charles Cameron might have given her the tenancy of Inch Cottage, but she provided for the rest of her double life entirely by herself. Other than in her devotion to your grandfather she was a fiercely independent lady.'

He held up his hand in mock-surrender. 'If that's true, I beg her pardon—and yours, Flora. She obviously meant a great deal to you.'

'She did.' Flora subsided, her eyes softening. 'The personality which enslaved your grandfather flourished until the day Aunt Jenny died. She was irreverent and witty, acid, frank, and far more fun than most of my contemporaries. I used to stay with her in her flat in Bloomsbury—a wonderful place, crammed with books and pictures and lots of eccentric friends.' She sighed deeply. 'I miss her so much.

Sometimes it seems hard to believe I won't see her again, more so since I've come here.' She smiled wryly. 'How she must have enjoyed hugging her secret about this place! My family fondly believed it was some little hut in the wilds.'

James frowned. 'You mean you knew nothing about Inch Cottage until you came here?'

'Not a clue. It was her little joke—I could almost hear her laughing when I first saw that room upstairs.'

'Which room?'

'Her bedroom, of course.' She smiled in surprise. 'Have you never seen it?'

'Uncharted territory to me.' He eyed her quizzically. 'Why is it such a joke?'

Flora hesitated, then shrugged and got to her feet. 'I suppose there's no harm in seeing for yourself. You'll find a friend.'

James followed her from the room, intrigued. 'Who?'

She went ahead of him up the staircase and opened the door to the bedroom with a flourish. '*Voilà*!'

James stopped dead on the threshold, his eyes widening incredulously as the lush, erotic room made the inevitable impact. He whistled softly.

'Good grief! I'm surprised there's no mirror on the ceiling.'

'Plenty in here,' said Flora, opening the bathroom door.

James shook his head, grinning as he took a look inside. 'The old lecher! There's nothing remotely like this at Ardlochan.'

'I rather think that's the point of it.'

But James was gazing intently at his grandfather's portrait. The hard planes of his face softened as he met the eyes in the drawing.

'Hell, she was clever,' he said gruffly. 'That's him to the life. He never altered very much. He was as upright as a boy almost to the day he died—tall and fierce and worth two of any other man I've ever met.'

'Aunt Jenny thought the same. You had more in common with her than you realised.'

'I hardly knew her. Once my grandfather died the only person Miss Lyon had any contact with when she came was Jean MacPhail.' He shook his head as he gazed round him at the décor. 'What a *room*!'

Flora nodded. 'I felt a bit embarrassed at first in that bed.'

James eyed it appreciatively. 'It's pretty obvious what went on in it. And I'm glad. He deserved all the happiness he could get. It's common knowledge that my grandmother was an old dragon.'

'When did she die?'

'A week or so after her husband. My mother swears she hung on out of spite, just to make sure he never married Miss Lyon.'

Flora shivered as she went downstairs ahead of him. 'Did your grandmother ever come here?'

'Never. She refused to acknowledge it even existed. Besides, she spent the last twenty years of her life in France, much to my mother's relief.' He grimaced as they went back into the kitchen. 'Mother insisted I paid an occasional visit to her there, of course, because Grandmère was fond of me, believe it or not.'

'I do believe it.' Flora looked at him closely. 'Was your father fair?'

'Oh, yes, every inch a Cameron.' He smiled. 'The sole reason for Grandmère's partiality to me was my resemblance to *her* side of the family, barring the eyes.'

'Which are exactly like your grandfather's!'

He nodded. 'And how about you? Do you follow Miss Lyon for looks?'

'So I'm told.'

James looked at her in silence for a moment. 'Little wonder,' he said without inflexion, 'that my grandfather was so besotted.'

Annoyed to discover she was breathless, Flora turned away to look through the window. 'The rain's clearing a little, I think.'

'My cue to leave, I take it,' he said drily, and shrugged into his raincoat. 'I'll come back for you about three-thirty.'

'No, indeed, I'll drive myself——'

'Parts of the road are under water after the overnight rain. You'll be safer with a four-wheel-drive.'

Flora inclined her head politely. 'In that case I'll avail myself of your offer. Please convey my thanks to your mother.'

'Don't I deserve thanks for bringing you the papers?' he demanded.

'Of course. I'm sorry. Thank you very much indeed. It was very kind of you to think of me.'

He smiled sardonically. 'Nothing kind about it. I lay awake thinking about you most of the night, Flora Blair, one way and another. See you later.' His smile deepened at the suspicion on her face, then he sprinted out to the Land Rover through the heavy rain, raising a hand in salute as he drove off towards the loch.

Flora went back indoors deep in thought. James's parting shot had been ambiguous. It was flattering to know he'd been thinking of her. But *how*, exactly? As an attractive woman, or merely an obstacle in his path as regarded

Inch Cottage? She frowned. It wouldn't do to let James Cameron loom too large on her horizon. There was no denying the attraction of the man, whatever his motives in cultivating her, but it would be madness to get involved with someone she'd never see again once she left Ardlochan. In a few days she'd be gone, and after she'd returned the tenancy of Inch Cottage to its owner she'd have no reason to come back here again. Not, of course, that she'd want to. Not really. It was a beautiful place when the sun was shining, but very forbidding when sullen grey clouds hung low like today. For weather like this one needed company at Inch Cottage, preferably that of a lover like Aunt Jenny's.

Flora halted her train of thought abruptly. What on earth was the matter with her? Steeping herself in a long-dead romance was addling her wits! Besides, if James Cameron really had any idea about history repeating itself he could think again. A spot of illicit romance might have been all very well for a woman of Aunt Jenny's era and situation, but there were a great many more options open to a woman these days than in Genista Lyon's youth.

Nevertheless, when James arrived, prompt to the minute at three-thirty, Flora's hair was no longer pulled back in a braid, but tied loosely at the nape of her neck with a silk scarf, tendrils left loose to curl at her ears. And her cream linen shirt and skirt were more products of her French wardrobe.

'Very elegant,' commented James, leaping down from the vehicle.

Flora eyed the sky from the open doorway. 'Thank you. I wasn't sure your mother would appreciate a visitor in jeans and sneakers for Sunday tea, but they'd be a lot more practical in this rain.' She shrugged into her old ski-jacket, pulled the hood up over her hair and locked the door behind her.

James eyed the narrow skirt speculatively. 'I'd better give you a boost-up.' He seized her by the elbows and tossed her up into the passenger seat. 'Right, then, Miss Blair, let's away.'

Flora found herself enjoying James Cameron's company rather more than she felt was wise as he talked about the estate, and the forestry work taking place on part of it.

'We run our timber business as a co-operative,' he informed her. 'The exotic woods are sold off, the other stuff is processed in our own sawmills for fencing and so on, and everyone on the estate enjoys a free supply of firewood.'

Flora chuckled. 'Including me?'

'Especially you—now I've met you.' He gave her a sudden, sidelong grin. 'Though to be honest it would take a braver man than me to refuse logs to Jean MacPhail for Inch Cottage or anywhere else!'

When they reached Ardlochan House James led the way to a smaller, shabbier room than the formal apartments of the evening before. In defiance of summer a fire burned cheerfully in a small, cast-iron fireplace, with comfortable chintz-covered chairs drawn up close to it. Vases of flowers stood on tables and cabinets alongside framed photographs, a partly worked tapestry spilled from a work-basket alongside an open book on the sofa. As James took Flora's jacket his mother came hurrying into the room, two elderly retrievers panting behind her.

'I'm sorry, my dear,' she said, smiling. 'I decided to take these ladies for a walk while there was a lull in the downpour.'

Flora greeted her hostess a little shyly, secretly thankful she'd made an effort with her appearance. Isobel Cameron's tailored blouse and skirt were plain enough, but she wore pearls in her ears, and her hair was so immaculate that she'd obviously taken time to tidy herself up on her way in from her walk.

'It was very good of you to ask me to tea so soon, Mrs Cameron,' said Flora, stooping to fondle the friendly dogs.

'I'm away to Edinburgh tomorrow, and as it's such a dreary day today it seemed like a good idea. You'd hardly be out sketching in this rain.' Mrs Cameron gave her tall son a smile. 'Do go away, James. Tie trout flies, or catch up on the paperwork you complain about so much.'

He looked aggrieved. 'Am I not allowed any tea, then?'

'In an hour,' said his mother firmly, and with a shrug and a smile James strolled from the room, leaving Flora to bear Isobel Cameron's thoughtful scrutiny. After a moment or two Mrs Cameron nodded slowly.

'With time to study you at my leisure I see a definite resemblance to Miss Lyon.'

Flora smiled. 'I know. There are several photographs of her at home at my age.'

'And how old is that, my dear?'

'I'm twenty-six.'

'You surprise me. You look younger.' Mrs Cameron shooed the dogs away from the fire. 'I hear you're an art teacher, just like Miss Lyon in her younger days.'

Flora nodded. 'It was she who encouraged my artistic leanings. We had a very close relationship; the age-difference never seemed to matter.'

'Which is why she gave Inch Cottage into your keeping, of course.' Mrs Cameron smiled. 'It came as something of a shock to James, I'm afraid.'

'So I gather.'

'He's been waiting so long—and patience is not his strong suit—for it to revert to him, you see. There was nothing he could do while Miss Lyon was alive.' The dark eyes danced suddenly. 'And indeed there is nothing he can do now you've arrived on the scene, Miss Blair. Or may I call you Flora?'

'Of course.' Suddenly Flora felt horribly guilty. The only thing which kept her from relieving Mrs Cameron's anxiety about Inch Cottage was the fact that she'd be doing the same for James. And she had no intention of letting *him* off her hook. Not yet, anyway.

Mrs Cameron made no more mention of Inch Cottage. She drew Flora out on the subject of her family and her career instead, then responded in kind with a thumbnail sketch of life at Ardlochan.

'We are a little remote here, but I wouldn't live anywhere else,' she confided. 'If things had been different I think your great-aunt would have been happy to spend her entire life here, too.'

'It must have been an odd situation for you—her annual visit, I mean,' said Flora.

'By the time I came here as a bride it was already an old-established custom, and so much a part of life at Ardlochan I just accepted it. Besides,' added Mrs Cameron, 'I liked Miss Lyon, what little I was allowed to know of her. The old laird guarded her fiercely, while his wife, of course, never acknowledged her existence by so much as a flicker of an eyelash.' She shrugged. 'I'm not giving away family secrets when I say my husband's mother was always a stranger to me. She spent so little time here at Ardlochan, I never came to know her very well, and eventually she retired permanently to her family home in France.'

'From the letter Aunt Jenny left me I gathered the lady would never have chosen to marry and leave France in the first place——' Flora checked, colouring. 'Which is absolutely none of my business.'

'Nonsense.' Mrs Cameron smiled wryly. 'Honorine Cameron made no secret of the fact that given the choice she'd have entered a convent, which was why the marriage was a total disaster. Besides, my dear, in the circumstances I'm afraid you're involved with us whether you like it or not. Miss Lyon was the love of Charles Cameron's life, and he made no secret of it. He told her she could do as she wished with Inch Cottage, and since she chose to pass the tenancy to you you're perfectly entitled to keep it for your own use indefinitely.'

'I don't think your son shares your view on the subject.'

'James is cursed with the formidable Cameron temper—and the news came as a shock. Could I ask you to make allowances for him?'

Flora smiled wryly. 'I'll try.'

'Good.' Mrs Cameron rose to her feet briskly. 'Now, let me give you some tea. James and I look after ourselves on Sundays. Being a good, provident Scot I used up leftovers from last night's dinner for lunch, but my Agnes has left us one of her orange and almond cakes and I made some scones, so we'll do very well at teatime.'

'After the meal I ate last night I thought I'd never be hungry again,' said Flora with feeling.

Mrs Cameron chuckled and excused herself to go off to the kitchen. A moment later James entered the room with a laden tray and set it down on a table near his mother's place on the sofa.

'I thought you'd never stop talking,' he said, and stood with his back to the fire, looking down at Flora. 'Well? Is your opinion of Highland hospitality gradually improving?'

'By leaps and bounds!' She met the bright silver gaze with a quizzical look. 'Though I can't help wondering why my landlord seems so much better disposed towards me now than at first.'

James smiled crookedly. 'At that first meeting I wasn't ill-disposed to *you* in particular, it was just that I felt such a bloody fool. And the second time we met I'd just heard about the tenancy—I was battling with my temper.'

'And losing,' she pointed out.

He conceded the hit. 'I shouldn't have taken it out on you, I know.' He raised an eyebrow. 'Am I forgiven?'

Mrs Cameron's reappearance spared Flora a reply, as conversation became general, both Camerons interested in their visitor's explorations of the area.

'I haven't got very far at all yet,' confessed Flora. 'I take my sketchbook with me, which means I never get any distance before I find something I just have to get down on paper— that ruined tower near by for one.' She explained how it had captured her imagination so much that she was making several studies of it in charcoal.

James exchanged a glance with his mother. 'Then you must come here to view it from the best angle. It's all that remains of what was once the ancestral home of this branch of the Camerons. The present house is relatively modern.'

Flora smiled in delight. 'I was sure it had something to do with Ardlochan the moment I set eyes on it. Can one go inside?'

'Only with great care,' warned Mrs Cameron. 'James will show you round, but never try exploring it by yourself. For one thing it's not safe, and for another——'

'It's haunted,' said James with relish, and handed Flora a dish of scones.

'By what—or whom?' she asked, fascinated.

'The ghost of a medieval Cameron lady. While her husband was away on crusade a neighbouring laird falsely reported him dead and laid siege to the place, determined to possess both tower and châtelaine. But she killed herself rather than surrender.'

'What happened to the husband?'

James shrugged. 'The usual thing. He came home, killed the usurper, married again and produced several sons to succeed him. But the

ghost of Lady Mariotta still haunts the tower—
so it's said.'

Mrs Cameron frowned in disapproval as she
refilled Flora's cup. 'It's just a legend. I've been
there many a time, and never seen a thing.'

'Ah,' said James solemnly, 'but have you ever
climbed to the top when the moon is full,
Mother?'

'No,' she said acidly. 'And anyone who does
must be soft in the head. These days the only
way you can get up to the very top is by ladder.'

'But the view when you get there is unri-
valled.' James smiled at Flora. 'No artist worth
her salt would balk at a mere bit of a scramble
to see it.'

'That sounds like a challenge,' she observed,
buttering a scone.

'Pay no heed to him, Flora,' said Mrs
Cameron firmly. 'By all means visit the place,
but make sure you go in broad daylight.'

'I'll take you tomorrow, if you like,' James
offered.

Flora stared at him in surprise. 'Why, how
kind.'

'Unless you've something better to do, of
course.'

'No. Nothing. If the weather's fine I'd like that very much—if you can spare the time.'

'An hour or so out of my day won't bring the estate to a standstill,' he assured her blandly.

CHAPTER FIVE

FLORA spent a restless night after her tea party at Ardlochan. James had driven her home, seen her into the house then driven away again, with a promise to be back for her in the morning, as casually friendly as though his original hostility had been a figment of her imagination.

But she knew very well it had not, and felt deeply suspicious of James Cameron complete with olive-branch. Not that he need put himself out to gain his ends, she told herself, giving her pillow a vicious thump. In a day or so she would hand Inch Cottage on a plate to the laird of Ardlochan and take off for France, and that would be that. But in the meantime she would make good use of the olive-branch by exploring the tower with the best guide possible—the man who owned it.

Next morning it was still raining. Flora viewed the weather with a jaundiced eye and abandoned all hope of a trip to the tower with James. Irritated by the depth of her disappointment, she indulged in an energetic burst of tidying up to counteract it, and had almost recovered when the expected knock came on the front door. She ran downstairs, reminding herself that James had come in person solely because Inch Cottage lacked a phone. She threw open the door, her eyes widening as instead of James Cameron she found Ewen Urquhart holding an umbrella over his sister, who looked so sensational in brief tartan shorts and yellow cashmere T-shirt that Flora deeply regretted the faded jeans and elderly jersey she'd chosen as appropriate wear for exploring a ruin.

'Good morning. What a lovely surprise,' lied Flora, smiling. 'Do come in.'

'We were just passing,' said Catriona, and strolled into the hall, her green eyes avidly curious as she looked around.

Ewen smiled awkwardly as he stowed the umbrella in a tall Chinese jar near the door. 'Nice to see you, Miss Blair. I hope we've not come at an awkward time?'

Flora assured her visitors she was delighted, and led them into the parlour. 'Coffee?' she enquired.

'No, thanks, can't stay,' said Catriona, ignoring her brother's obvious disappointment. 'Ewen found there was no phone here at the lodge and insisted on driving over to deliver an invitation.' She gave Flora a feline smile. 'I just came along for the ride.'

Ewen handed her an envelope, an eager smile on his face. 'It's from my mother. For Cat's birthday dance.'

Flora opened the envelope, astonished to find that she was, indeed, invited to attend a dance at Strathroy, home of the Urquharts, the following Friday.

'Short notice, of course,' said Ewen uneasily, eyeing her face. 'But do come. You'll enjoy it—lots of reels and so on, but a bit of a disco as well.'

'It's wonderfully kind of your mother to invite me,' said Flora gently, 'and very nice of you both to deliver it, but——'

'Oh, nothing to do with me,' yawned Catriona, turning from her inspection of the water-colours. 'Ewen's idea entirely. There'll be loads of people there. One more won't make any difference, I suppose.'

Flora put the envelope down on a table. 'Thank you, but I'm leaving soon, probably before your dance.'

Unlike his sister, who brightened openly at the news, Ewen looked bitterly disappointed. 'Surely you can hang on long enough to come to Cat's dance! We'd be delighted if you would,' he added, avoiding his sister's eye.

Flora hadn't the heart to turn him down flat. 'Perhaps you could let me think about it for a while. Could I defer my answer for a day or so?'

'Oh, fine,' he said, beaming. 'As long as you like. And don't worry about transport—I'll come and fetch you. Only too pleased——' A peremptory rapping on the main door interrupted him.

Flora found James on the doorstep, eyeing Ewen's car. He gave her a brief greeting then asked why Ewen was there.

'Come in and ask him,' said Flora. 'We're in the parlour.'

James strode into the room, then stopped short at the sight of both Urquharts, and looked from one to the other, eyebrows raised. 'What brings you two here at this time of day?'

'They came to see me,' said Flora very distinctly. 'Why don't we have some coffee?'

'I didn't expect to find *you* here, James,' said Catriona, pouting. 'We were about to call in at Ardlochan.'

'Sorry,' said James, shrugging. 'I'm here to take Miss Blair to the tower. She's keen to see the view from the top——'

'Not that keen,' interrupted Flora. 'By all means go back with your friends. I can see the tower some other time.'

James gave her an impatient look. 'Possibly. But I can't. My time's not my own during the week.'

'Look, we'll push off,' said Ewen hastily. 'We only came to deliver an invitation to Cat's dance, James. Must get back for lunch.'

'It's not vital,' contradicted Catriona. She smiled cajolingly at James. 'Why don't we *all* go to the tower?'

He laughed. 'Dressed like that?'

Catriona eyed Flora up and down. 'Perhaps Miss Blair could lend me something—or perhaps not,' she amended sweetly. 'She's so much taller than me.'

'Thinner too,' agreed Flora, equally saccharine.

Ewen took his sister firmly by the arm. 'We'll leave you to it. Come on, Cat. Goodbye, Miss Blair. Please stay for the dance.'

Flora smiled non-committally as the four of them moved into the hall.

Catriona waved a denigratory hand at her surroundings. 'I must say this place is a great disappointment—so austere. Nothing like a love-nest after all.'

James carefully avoided Flora's eye as he went to see off the Urquharts. When he returned to the house Flora closed the door and went off to the kitchen.

James followed her. 'I didn't expect to find those two here.'

'Neither did I.' She smiled faintly. 'At the risk of sounding conceited I think Ewen came to see me, but Catriona's motive was less clear. Curiosity about Inch Cottage, perhaps, topped off by a visit to you on the way back.'

'You don't like Catriona, I gather.'

'The boot's on the other foot. *She* doesn't like *me*.'

'Which makes it all the more extraordinary that she invited you to her dance,' James commented.

'She didn't. Ewen was behind that.'

'You've obviously made a conquest.'

'Ewen's a very nice man...' she said elliptically. 'But how he persuaded Catriona to part with an invitation I can't imagine. I must be the last person she wanted on her guest-list.'

James perched himself on a corner of the table, swinging a long, khaki-clad leg. 'Will you go?'

'I doubt it. I'll probably be gone by then.'

His eyes narrowed. 'So soon?'

'I haven't decided yet. Coffee?'

'Thank you. Time for one cup then we can get off to the tower.'

Flora stared. 'In this weather?'

'I guarantee clear skies in under half an hour.'

'You're joking.'

He shook his sleek, damp head. 'Fancy a wager?'

She went over to the window to scan the sullen grey sky, then turned to him with a grin. 'You're on!'

James looked at the clock. 'Right. It's ten-thirty. If the rain hasn't cleared by eleven I buy you dinner tonight. If it does...' He paused.

She eyed him suspiciously. 'Go on.'

He grinned, looking suddenly younger. 'I've got half an hour to think of something appropriate. Let's wait and see.'

The wait was short. To Flora's astonishment the sun was shining from an almost clear sky after a mere fifteen minutes. She stared from the window at the glittering loch, then at James in accusation. 'You heard a weather forecast!'

'I didn't need one. I was born here, remember.' He moved to join her at the window. 'Now it's settling-up time.'

To her annoyance Flora felt her heart give a thump. 'What did you have in mind?'

James's eyes scanned her face, something in their expression bringing the blood rushing to her cheeks.

'You're blushing,' he informed her, a remark which did nothing to alleviate the problem.

'Just tell me what you want,' she snapped, looking away.

'Nothing too difficult. I just thought I'd keep to my original idea. Your company at dinner tonight.'

Flora, suffering somewhat from anticlimax, was almost tempted to refuse, but curiosity got the better of her. 'Why?'

His eyebrows rose. 'Must there be a reason? As I said, I would like your company. What's so strange about that?'

'The fact that it's a bit of a volte-face on your part,' she said frankly. 'A few days ago you were ready to run me off your land. Now the olive-branches keep coming, thick and fast. You can't blame a poor, simple Sassenach like me for being suspicious.'

'What are men usually after when they ask you out to dinner?' he demanded.

Flora shrugged. 'That depends. Whatever it is they rarely get anything other than conversation and the pleasure of my company.'

He eyed her sardonically. 'Which is all *I'm* asking for, believe it or not. So what's it to be—yes, or no?'

She looked at him consideringly for a moment or two. 'Oh, why not? Yes, thank you. Dinner would be very pleasant.'

'Don't overwhelm me with enthusiasm,' he said drily. 'Now let's away. I happen to have work to do today, as well as jaunting off to the tower with you, Miss Blair.'

Flora had enjoyed her forays along the shores of the loch to the full with only her sketchbook for company. But with James Cameron for guide the drama and beauty of the area took on an entirely new dimension. Once they left Inch Cottage behind she decided to ignore the fact that it remained an obstinate bone of contention between them. For the time being she would forget that James Cameron was her unwilling landlord and look on him merely as an interesting companion, a role he filled admirably. As he pointed out each striking feature of his birthplace she felt she was seeing the loch and the woods and the towering slopes of the glen with new eyes, every detail of the scene more sharply defined as the sun glittered on wet green leaves and blue satin water. Flora gave a deep sigh of pleasure as she gazed through the windscreen of the Land Rover.

'This is a truly magnificent place,' she remarked. 'It's easy to see why Aunt Jenny loved it so much.'

'Perhaps her feeling for my grandfather had something to do with that,' James suggested.

'Possibly.' Flora turned to look at him. 'But then, she only visited for a short period every year. Perhaps if she'd spent her entire life in Ardlochan her passion for it might have diminished.'

'You think that would happen if you lived here?'

Flora shrugged. 'Since I'm not likely to I'll never know.'

'True.' James concentrated on a particularly narrow stretch of road, drawing over in courteous Highland fashion at one point for a car to pass safely. 'Tell me about yourself.'

'What, in particular?'

'Men, I suppose.' He glanced at her hand. 'No ring, but that doesn't mean anything. Do you share your life with someone?'

Flora hesitated for a moment. 'I have a special friend who happens to be male. He's a commercial artist. But I don't exactly share my life with him.'

'Have you done so with anyone else?'

'I was engaged once,' she admitted.

'May I ask what happened?'

'He's an army man who married the colonel's daughter instead.'

James threw her a searching glance. 'When was this?'

'Years ago, when I was a student. I was invited to a dinner party at Sandhurst. Nicholas was there, gorgeous in his scarlet and black, and I was a naïve young maiden. I was so beglamoured I was ready to turn my back on teaching, and become a good little army wife instead.' Flora smiled cheerfully. 'Fortunately Nick's timing was excellent. He ditched me so quickly I hadn't had time to refuse my college place. Aunt Jenny took me off to stay with her in Bloomsbury to lick my wounds until term started, then I just got on with the rest of my life. How about you?' she added abruptly.

James shrugged. 'I'm the usual, normal male; I like the company of women. But enjoying the odd pleasurable encounter with a member of your sex is a far cry from settling down with one for life. I've dined with a good many ladies very happily, but breakfasting with one on a permanent basis holds no appeal at all—to date.' He swerved off on to a bumpy path that brought them to the edge of the loch, where the tower reared up starkly against the bright sky. 'Right, then, Flora Blair. Welcome to my tower.'

At close quarters the ancient pile of stones was more of a ruin than it appeared from a distance, but Flora found it no less fascinating for all that. She sprang down unaided from the

Land Rover and hurried towards the tower, which brooded almost at the water's edge, the topmost gaping window like an eye trained on the length of the loch for invaders.

'When it really was a watchtower whom would your ancestors have been guarding against?' she asked.

'Vikings, originally, then raiders from warring clans.' He smiled. 'We Scots are more peaceable these days.'

'I'm not sure I agree with that,' said Flora drily. 'Can we climb up inside?'

James cast an eye at her jeans and trainers, and nodded. 'I've set up a ladder, but promise you'll be careful.'

'I'm always careful!'

Inside the ruin, at the base of the tower where no sunlight ever penetrated, it was dank and musty, the atmosphere thick with dust and antiquity. Flora shivered involuntarily.

James eyed her quizzically. 'Are you sure you want to go up there?'

'Absolutely.'

'Right. Now your eyes are used to the light can you see the old steps leading up to the first floor? Be careful. They're worn and very uneven. I'll go first.'

Flora followed him up the ancient, crumbling steps through the gloom, relieved to find the light better when they reached the jagged apertures of windows that had never been glazed or shuttered against the cold.

'Brr!' Shivering as she paused on the wooden planking which floored part of the middle section of the building, she cast a doubtful eye at the ladder which provided the only means of access to the uppermost part of the tower.

'I'll foot the ladder while you climb—if you're still set on it, that is.'

Not for worlds would Flora have admitted she wasn't so keen now that she realised what the climb entailed. 'Ready when you are.'

She started gingerly up the rungs, glad of rubber-soled shoes which gripped securely. Then James settled his weight at the foot of the ladder and she felt safer. She climbed the remaining rungs slowly, her relief intense when she scrambled over the top on to the splintered planking which formed a bridge between the uppermost walls of the watchtower. She negotiated it with care and leaned, panting, on the jagged, crumbling stones of the window aperture.

'Well?' said James at her elbow. 'Was it worth it?'

Flora gazed in silence at cataracts creaming down amethyst hills mirrored in the shot-silk surface of the loch, which from this height looked like a jewel set in the gilded sand of the shore. She let out the breath she hadn't known she'd been holding. 'Worth it? James, it merits superlatives I can't even think of. Watercolour's not my usual medium, but I *must* try my hand at painting this. Will you give me permission? I promise I'll be careful. And of course I'd need a weather expert to tell me when the time was right.'

'I've no objection to your coming here, only to the risk involved in getting up here on your own. If you promise to let me bring you every time I suppose there's no harm in it.'

Her enthusiasm faded. 'But that's too much of an imposition. I couldn't possibly trouble you to that extent.'

'It would trouble me far more to think you were scrambling up here without my help!' He surveyed her thoughtfully. 'The weather's set fair for the next few days. I'll make a bargain. I bring you here as often as you like, you promise to stay on for Catriona Urquhart's dance.'

Flora stared at him in astonishment. '*You* want me to stay?'

His eyes met hers, as clear and uncommunicative as glass. 'Is that so hard to believe?'

'Frankly, yes.'

'I thought we'd declared a truce,' he reminded her. 'Surely it can hold out until then. Don't you like parties?'

'Of course I do—but not when the invitation's given under duress!' Flora looked him in the eye. 'Catriona obviously sees me as some kind of competition.'

'She wouldn't if she saw you now,' said James drily. He brushed her cheek with impersonal fingers. 'Your face is filthy and your hair's coming unravelled. A good thing your pupils aren't around, schoolma'am.'

'You don't look too wonderful yourself,' returned Flora tartly, then smiled hastily, remembering she needed his help. 'I won't trouble you much. I can drive myself to Ardlochan, then all you need do is follow me here and help me up the ladder in the morning and down again later on whenever it suits you.'

'Done.' He glanced at his watch. 'Time we were off. I'd better put in some work this afternoon. I'll go down first. Take great care as you follow.'

Flora found the descent rather more difficult than the climb up, and couldn't hide her relief when they reached ground level to emerge into the sunlight once more. She cast a yearning look over her shoulder as they returned to the car, vious. You've looked in a mirror lately, I imagine?'

Flora studied him in silence for a moment. 'Ah, I see. If my appearance had been less to your taste you'd still be waging war on my tenancy of Inch Cottage—not that I think you've *stopped* waging war by any means. I fancy you've just changed your tactics.'

His laugh sent trickles down her spine. 'Is it so obvious? But you're right. I'm an honest man, Flora, so I have no choice but to admit that after tonight warfare is the last thing on my mind where you're concerned. Unless, of course, I throw caution to the winds and try my hand at laying siege to your heart.'

Flora went scarlet, deeply thankful that the light was too poor for him to see. It was almost a relief to see Catriona materialise through the dusk to lay a possessive hand on James's arm.

'Your mother sent me to say the Drummonds are ready to leave.' She smiled smugly at Flora. 'Goodnight, Miss Blair. Safe journey.'

wishing she'd brought her paints with her to start straight away.

'The tower's been there a long time, it won't run away,' James assured her, reading her mind.

'Ah, but will the weather hold?'

'I'll lay odds on it.'

Flora gave him a wry look as they drove off. 'I'm not getting involved in any more bets with you, Mr Cameron.'

'Talking of which,' he said, 'I'll come and pick you up about seven-thirty or so.'

'No need. I'll drive over to your place and save you part of the journey.'

He gave her a scathing look. 'I don't know what barbarian Sassenach customs you're used to, but in this neck of the woods, Miss Blair, we see a lady safely home when we take her out.'

Flora subsided, routed, and changed the subject, curious about the exact role the laird played on the estate of Ardlochan. To her surprise she learned that James was his own factor.

'I'm a hard-working estate manager, with a great deal of help from men like Donald MacPhail, who've lived here all their lives and know the place like the palms of their hands,' he told her. 'When I reached the age of wondering what to do with my life my grandfather suggested I take a degree in land management ready for the day when Ardlochan became my sole responsibility.'

'Strange really,' mused Flora, as Inch Cottage came in sight. 'You had Charles Cameron helping to shape your life, and I had his beloved Genista doing the same for me, yet neither of us knew the other existed until a short time ago.'

'We do now,' said James, coming to a halt. 'I hope the discovery hasn't jaundiced your opinion of Scotland!'

'Of course not,' she answered lightly. 'No— don't get out. After scrambling up and down that ladder like a monkey on a stick I'm more than capable of hopping down from your car.'

He smiled, and raised a hand in salute. 'I'll see you later, then.'

Flora waved him off then hurried to turn on the taps in the mirror-lined bathroom, light-hearted at the thought of the evening ahead. Convinced that his sole intention was to soften her up on the subject of Inch Cottage, she was still human enough to look forward to dining with a man as formidably attractive as James Cameron.

The afternoon was so beautiful that Flora decided to take full advantage of the weather after her bath and indulged in a little sun-bathing. She lay supine on a rug on the lawn, hair spread out to dry, as she wondered where James would take her to dine. To what lengths was the laird of Ardlochan prepared to go? she wondered, smiling to herself. Quite a joke, really, to think he was prepared to spend time, effort and money on wining and dining her to gain his ends, when in a few days the house would be his and all his effort proved unnecessary. From her slight acquaintance with the charismatic Mr Cameron there was no doubt he'd be annoyed. Which would serve him right. If he'd been less belligerent to start with, victory would have been his long since.

When James arrived that evening Flora was impressed. If he'd set out to charm he'd made a very good beginning with his appearance alone, she conceded. His eyes seemed to gleam more brilliantly than usual against his tawny skin and soot-black hair, and in deference to the warmth of the evening he wore light linen trousers and a pale pink shirt that on another man might have smacked of femininity, but on James Cameron merely emphasised his maleness.

'A paragon among women,' he commented, his own admiration clear in his eyes for her to see. 'You're ready. I thought I might have to kick my heels for half an hour, studying my inherited water-colours.'

'Your experience of women has obviously made you cynical,' remarked Flora, letting out an inelegant whistle at the sight of the old, lovingly polished Aston Martin standing in front of the house.

'I use this strictly for special occasions,' he announced, handing her into the passenger seat. 'And tonight is more special than usual. I'm rarely blessed with so beautiful a passenger.'

Flora, who had taken a quite outrageous length of time to create a good impression, smiled, suspicious of his flattery, but fully aware that she looked her best in the dress bought for hot summer evenings in the Perigord. Made of thin, floating lawn, the muted topaz-yellow shade did wonders for the glow acquired from her session in the sun.

'Thank you, though I imagine mere cleanliness would be an improvement on the way I looked earlier on.'

'It would be impossible to improve on the way you look now!'

Flora looked away. 'Shouldn't we be leaving?'

He laughed under his breath then started up the purring engine and drove down the track to the loch, which lay glittering under the deepening blue of the sky.

'On an evening like this it's hard to believe I woke up to rain and grey skies this morning,' she said, in an effort to dispel the hint of intimacy in the air. 'This loch of yours seems to change its mood at the drop of a hat.'

'It won't for the next few days. The weather's set fair for at least a week.'

'I hope you're right. I'd dearly love to capture the view from the tower before—before I leave.'

'You've promised to stay for the Urquhart dance,' he reminded her.

Flora wrinkled her nose. 'Which was rash. The role of unwanted guest lacks appeal.'

'*Ewen* wants you. So do I.' He directed a gleaming, sidelong glance at her. 'You'd have a wonderful time, I promise. We know how to enjoy ourselves in this part of the world.'

'I'm sure you do——' Her eyes narrowed as she realised they were on the same familiar route which girdled the loch, the road she'd travelled twice already that day. 'Where are we eating, as a matter of interest?'

James stared straight ahead. 'I hope you won't be too disappointed if we just dine at Ardlochan. Do you object?'

Flora eyed his profile narrowly. 'I suppose not,' she said after a while.

'Ah! You feel you've wasted the effort taken to make yourself so ravishing.'

'It wasn't that difficult!' she said acidly, then caught his teasing eye and laughed. 'Actually, I might not have bothered *quite* so much for an audience of one. After all you've seen me at my worst, so any improvement on this afternoon would have done.'

'Instead you're a sight to ravish the eye, Flora Blair.' He brought the car to a halt with a flourish in front of Ardlochan House, where a table on the terrace waited, complete with silver and crystal and glass-shaded candles in readiness for the dark.

'We're dining al fresco!' she exclaimed in delight, stooping to pet the dogs who came frisking about her legs in welcome. 'What a lovely idea.' An oddly reassuring one.

Flora was even more reassured when a plump, bustling lady emerged from the house with a covered dish, her face wreathed in smiles as James introduced his guest as the new tenant of Inch Cottage.

'This is Mistress Agnes MacPhail, Flora,' announced James. 'She rules us with a rod of iron.'

'Och, away with ye, Mr James,' said Agnes, and put down the dish alongside several others on the table. 'I'm pleased to meet you, Miss Blair. Jean told me you were coming.'

Flora smiled warmly. 'You're related to the MacPhails?'

'I am Donald's sister, Miss Blair.'

'Of course! I can see the likeness.'

'But Donald's as quiet and reserved as our Agnes is the reverse,' said James, grinning, and put his arm around the indignant housekeeper. 'Don't be angry, Agnes, *mo cridhe*.'

Agnes bridled, scolding gently as she issued a flood of instructions about the meal, then said goodnight and took herself off.

'Normally she lives in,' said James as he seated Flora in a chair facing the sunlit water. 'But her old father isn't very well, so with Donald and Jean away in Perth, and my mother in Edinburgh, I told her to spend as much time with the old man as possible. I had a fight to convince her we could serve ourselves, but I won in the end, mainly because she's worried about old Donald.'

'You shouldn't have made her provide a meal,' said Flora. 'You could have taken me for a hamburger somewhere.' She smiled wickedly at the distaste on his face.

'Hardly likely! Tell me what you'd like to drink. I seem to remember a liking for single malt. A dram to start, perhaps?'

'Not before the meal. Later perhaps.'

The meal was a long, leisurely affair. James anticipated Flora's every wish with a flattering attention which heightened her enjoyment of an evening already atmospheric from the sheer beauty of the setting as they watched the sun sink to the far shoreline of the loch in a glory of gold and crimson.

'This is much better than any restaurant,' she told him.

'Thank you.' James smiled. 'Agnes had grave doubts about a cold meal, but I convinced her that it was exactly what you'd prefer on a night like this.'

Flora, who had worked her way through smoked trout pâté, thin slices of rare roast beef and various beautifully presented salads, agreed fervently, then insisted on helping him take the remains of the meal into the house, where she paused in awe on the threshold of the Ardlochan kitchen. By comparison the kitchen at Inch Cottage was a mere pantry.

'Good heavens! This place could cater for an army.'

He nodded, looking about him with affection as he helped her stow plates of leftovers in the refrigerator, and drop titbits in the dogs' bowls. 'It often did at one time. Previous generations of Camerons prided themselves on their hospitality. During September the place was always buzzing, right up to my grandfather's heyday. These days we entertain on a more modest scale.' He took out a bowl of ripe raspberries and a jug of cream. 'This is our pudding. Or you can have cheese. Or both.'

Flora opted for the fruit.

'We could stay inside to eat it if you'd prefer,' suggested James.

'No,' she answered, rather too quickly. 'Let's go back to the terrace with the dogs—please.'

'Whatever you say.' His eyes lingered on her bare arms and throat. 'Though be warned, the midges may nibble.'

She shook her head. 'I don't think so. My skin doesn't attract insects.'

'Hard to believe. It has the reverse effect on a mere male like me!'

Flora, annoyed to find herself slightly rattled, smiled politely. 'I'll make coffee, if you'll show me where everything is.'

James shook his head. 'Certainly not. You're my guest. If you can find your way back to the terrace, I'll see to the coffee. Agnes has given me full instructions.'

'Don't tell me you've never made coffee before!'

'I can pour boiling water on the instant stuff with the best of them, but my mother was given a complicated bit of machinery for Christmas last year and only Agnes seems to know how to make it work. But tonight,' he said very softly, meeting her eyes, 'I'm set on conquest. So just commune with nature outside for a few minutes, Flora, and I'll be with you.'

Lying back in a chair on the terrace with the dogs at her feet, Flora stared at the darkening sky, no longer relaxed as she wondered if the conquest in question would be limited to the coffee-machine. Her mouth tightened. James Cameron was an attractive man by any standards, but if he expected a session in bed to round off the evening's entertainment he'd be disappointed. She looked up with a start as James reappeared, triumphant, bearing a tray.

'The instructions were crystal-clear once I'd deciphered Agnes's handwriting,' he announced smugly. 'You pour, Flora, while I go back for the Glenlivet—unless you'd care to change your mind tonight and have some cognac?'

'Just coffee will be fine for the moment.'

Flora filled their cups, then sat erect in her chair, her eyes on the sliver of moon which hung like a charm from the ribbon of turquoise light on the horizon.

'A penny for them,' said James, his eyes on her face.

'I was thinking how lucky you are to live in such an idyllic place.'

'Idyllic it may be, but unlike Eden it lacks a certain ingredient to make it perfect.'

'What, exactly?'

He gave her a mocking smile. 'A companion, of course. Even Eden must have seemed flat to Adam until Eve arrived on the scene. But enough about this place. Tell me about yours. Do you still live with your parents?'

'I teach at a boarding-school, which takes care of the major part of the year. Otherwise my bedroom's always waiting for me at home, in a Gloucestershire village where most people have known me since I was born—or I occupy a spare bed in various places.'

'But not one in particular?'

'No. I have a lot of friends—of both sexes,' she said, determined not to let him needle her. 'The circle's growing smaller, I admit, due to marriage and other partnerships. The new partner is not always fond of the old friend.'

'If the new partner's a woman and you're the old friend, I can see the pitfalls!'

'Why?'

'You know why. Think of Catriona Urquhart's reaction to you for a start.'

Flora shrugged. 'I'm no threat to Catriona—nor to anyone else. I've got my life sorted out in exactly the way I like it.'

'Exclusive of durable relationships?'

Flora turned her head sharply, but James's face was a shadowy oval in the twilight, giving no clue to his thoughts. 'Oh, I didn't say that.' She got up. 'It's been a delightful evening, but it's late. I must go.'

James leapt to his feet. 'You haven't had your dram yet.'

'I think I'll pass on that.' She smiled up at him. 'I told you I should have driven myself here tonight. You'd have been spared the trouble of taking me home.'

'It's no trouble, Flora Blair. No trouble at all.' His teeth showed white in the darkness of his face.

'In that case,' she retorted, purposely brisk, 'let's be off. If you mean what you say about taking me to the tower I'd like to make an early start tomorrow—always supposing you're right about the weather.'

'Oh, ye of little faith. Tomorrow, I promise, will be sunny and warm. All day. If not you can wreak what revenge you like.'

'Be careful—I might!'

On the twilit drive along the deserted road, Flora began to feel tense. She'd been so sure

that at some stage James would put out feelers
about getting the house back, yet so far he
hadn't said a word. All his original hostility was
gone as if it have never been. In fact, he'd be-
haved all evening like a man whose only motive
in seeking her company was the simple fact that
he found her attractive, letting her know in
various subtle ways which almost lulled her into
forgetting that Inch Cottage stood between
them.

'That was a very heartfelt sigh,' commented
James, glancing at her profile.

'I was just drinking in the beauty of the
night,' she fibbed lightly.

When they arrived at Inch Cottage James
calmly took the key from her to unlock the
door, ushered her inside and closed the door
behind him.

'And just in case you intended to offer me
coffee,' he said, in a tone which started her
heart thumping, 'I think you should know I'm
in imminent danger of falling in love with you,
Flora Blair. All I want is this.' And without cer-
emony he took her in his arms and kissed her.

CHAPTER SIX

FLORA stiffened and tried to push him away, but James held her fast, silencing her protest with his invading tongue. One hard, muscular arm held her still while his free hand sought her breasts. Long, expert fingers caressed her through the thin lawn, igniting shameless response from nipples which rose, erect, to his touch. She stiffened, gasped, wrenched back her head, but he laughed, ignoring her struggles as he moved his lips down her throat in a glissade of kisses which halted at last, hot and demanding on the pulse which throbbed there. The blood pounded in her ears, almost deafening her as James moved his mouth lower, his hands suddenly impatient as they thrust aside her dress. His mouth closed over a hard nipple and a great shiver convulsed her entire body, and abruptly he swept her up in his arms, deaf to her frantic protests as he carried her struggling body up the stairs and through the door which stood ajar at the top.

James kicked it shut behind him and fell with her to the bed, pulling her against him with such implicit urgency that Flora, enraged, began to fight in earnest. But James Cameron was a man used to active, physical work, and held her still with hands which bruised.

'I want you,' he said against her mouth, his voice rough and uneven, the Highland lilt suddenly pronounced. Flora shook her head in wordless, violent opposition, and his face darkened as he stared down into hers. 'Why the resistance? Your beloved Aunt Jenny would never have been so coy, surely!'

At which Flora found the strength to free a hand and fetched the dark, mocking face a ringing blow across the mouth before she made a lunge for freedom to the far side of the bed. She jumped to her feet and stood erect, breathing in gasps as she raked back her hair from eyes blazing with contempt.

James rose to face her across the expanse of rumpled covers, his clenched fist pressed to his mouth. He took it away, eyeing the blood on his hand with a detachment Flora found deeply insulting, following hard on the heat and urgency of only seconds before. 'Violence was entirely unnecessary,' he said coldly. 'At any point all you had to do was say no.'

'I tried! You—you took no notice.' Flora's chin lifted haughtily. 'Next, I suppose, you'll say I asked for it merely by agreeing to spend the evening with you. But that's *all* I agreed to. There was never any question of—of all this!'

'Yet you responded to me at first,' he said harshly.

She gave a bitter little laugh. 'I'm not denying it. It was only when the going got rough that I objected. I never dreamed you'd expect more than a kiss or two, though I suppose I was an idiot not to, in *these* surroundings.' Flora bent to switch on one of the rose-shaded lamps, and at once the room sprang to life, assaulting the eye with its flagrant eroticism. She gave him a scathing look. 'But I'm not Genista Lyon, nor are you Charles Cameron. I suppose it's my fault for showing you this room in the first place. It obviously opened your eyes to the sexual nature of the relationship he enjoyed with the woman he loved. But the word, remember, is "loved". No one seeing this room could doubt that they loved each other in every way possible between a man and a woman.'

James folded his arms, eyeing her with hostility. 'So? What has all that to do with you— and me?'

'You were the one who mentioned falling in love,' she reminded him. 'This room must have planted the idea in your head.'

He gave her a slow, derisive smile which brought her colour back with a rush. 'My dear girl, I'm a grown man, not some adolescent boy. You're on entirely the wrong track. In my experience, which is reasonably wide, women like a little gilding on the gingerbread when it comes to sex. It's much easier to gain access to a lady's bed if one talks first of love.' And with a mocking bow he turned on his heel and went from the room and out of the house.

Flora stood with clenched fists, rigid with outrage as the last echoes of James Cameron's departure faded into silence, then she stormed downstairs to bolt the front door.

Fighting for calm, she went to the kitchen, filled the kettle, made tea, sat at the table, and drained two cups in swift succession. Suddenly she banged her fist on the table in angry frustration. One thing was sure: she'd never paint the view from the tower now.

After a restless night Flora woke at first light, unsurprised to find the day fine, just as James had forecast. She had a bath, dressed, packed her clothes and stripped the bed, then began a systematic tidying of the house, still simmering with rage as she relived the scene of the night before. How dared James Cameron take it for granted she'd let him make love to her? Gritting her teeth, she worked even faster, every sinew strained for escape. She'd drive to Fort William, leave the MacPhails' car there at the designated garage, then catch the train to Glasgow and all points south. She'd fulfilled Aunt Jenny's wish. Now all she wanted was to get out of here. Fast.

Flora carried her suitcases downstairs and dumped them in the hall, then stiffened at the sound of the familiar Land Rover approaching the house. She threw open the door and waited, foot tapping, as James sprang down and came towards her. He looked haggard, as though his night had been as bad as hers, she noted with satisfaction.

'Ready?' he demanded.

'As it happens, yes,' she said, shrugging into her linen jacket. 'You just caught me.'

He frowned as he looked beyond her to the luggage in the hall. 'What the hell's this? Where are you going?'

'Away.'

'*Away*? We were going to the watchtower, in case you'd forgotten.'

Flora's eyes flashed angrily. 'After last night? You must be joking!'

Flora slung the strap of her bag over her shoulder. 'Since you are here I'll hand over the key for Jean MacPhail.' She gave him a brief, unsmiling nod. 'Thank you again for the tour of the tower. Now if I'm to make my train I'd better dash.'

James's hand clenched on the key, his dark-ringed eyes like ice. 'So you're determined to go.'

'I would have thought that was obvious. Perhaps you'd be kind enough to help me with my luggage.'

She marched out to the MacPhails' car, leaving James Cameron no option but to collect a pair of suitcases and follow her. In grim silence he loaded them into the boot then slammed down the lid with unnecessary force as she slid into the driving seat.

Flora looked up at him. 'Goodbye. Please give my regards to your mother.'

'Goodbye.' He bent suddenly, seized her face in hard, bruising hands and kissed her mouth. He released her even more abruptly, then turned on his heel, leapt into the Land Rover and gunned the engine mercilessly as he drove down the track to the loch. To her mortification Flora found her eyes were wet as she watched James Cameron drive out of her life, and after a moment or two she sniffed inelegantly and started the MacPhails' car.

To Flora's horror the engine gave a few dispirited whirring noises then died. Desperate now to be gone, she tried again, but with the same results. After several more attempts it was obvious the car was not going to start, and Flora gave a heartfelt groan before getting out to look under the bonnet. It was a token gesture. The sum total of her mechanical skill was knowing where to put in oil and water. Otherwise everything under the bonnet looked much the same as it always did—a coiled, incomprehensible mass.

And, thought Flora in despair, she'd handed over the key of the house to James. She slumped in the seat despondently for a while, wondering what to do, then jumped out of the car, immeasurably cheered by the sight of a small red van and the friendly, concerned face of Archie Lennox the postman as he came hurrying to see what was wrong.

When Flora explained her predicament Archie made a brief examination of the car and pronounced the battery flat. He deeply regretted his lack of jump-leads, but since he was on his way to Ardlochan he would call in on the laird and ask for help.

Flora thanked him with as good grace as possible, privately cursing her luck as she repaired to the rustic bench on the lawn to wait until help arrived. It was some time before it did. She was obliged to sit in the sunshine, seething and impatient, for the best part of an hour before the familiar Land Rover turned up the track to the house again.

'Problems?' enquired James curtly as he jumped out.

'Mr Lennox said the battery's flat.'

After a quick inspection James confirmed Archie's diagnosis. 'I don't have any jump-leads with me, but I can take the battery away and re-charge it for you.'

She stared at him in dismay. 'But I'll miss my train!'

'There'll be another tomorrow.'

Flora breathed in deeply. 'I *want* to go today. Is there a taxi available—or could *you* drive me to Fort William? I—I'd reimburse you, naturally.'

James gave her a look which flayed. 'Are you offering me *money*?'

'After your remarks last night I certainly didn't expect you to do it for love!' she snapped.

He fished in his pocket and produced the house key. 'Take my advice. Stay another day.

Even if we left now we'd never make the train. I'll return the battery in good time for you tomorrow.'

'But I'm all packed! What on earth am I to do with myself until then?'

James looked at her for a long, considering moment. 'You could always revert to the original plan and work at the tower.'

Flora opened her mouth to refuse, then thought better of it. Why not? It would pass the time. And she needn't use water-colour. She could make a charcoal sketch to complete her set. 'Are you sure it's convenient for you to take me there?' she asked formally.

James looked at his watch. 'If we leave in the next few minutes, yes. I'm due at the sawmill soon.'

After her luggage had been transferred to the house again Flora swiftly changed into jeans and sweatshirt, gathered up her equipment and ran to join James, who was waiting, very pointedly, outside in the garden.

'It's very civil of you to spare the time for this,' she said as they started off.

He shrugged indifferently. 'Since I'd already allowed for the expedition to the watchtower this morning it makes very little difference.'

Snubbed and smarting, Flora maintained a dignified silence for the rest of the journey.

When they arrived at the tower James took charge of her paraphernalia and waved her ahead of him up the worn stone steps to the first storey.

'You lead the way this time. I'll bring up the rear.'

'I could carry some of it myself——'

'You could also fall and break a leg,' he said impatiently.

Flora held her tongue, finding, in any case, that she needed all her energies for the arduous ascent, particularly on the ladder up to the vantage-point at the top of the tower. But the moment she was safe she forgot James and gazed, breathless and elated, at the panorama spread out like a feast before her hungry eyes.

'You're glad you came,' he stated drily, laying her easel beside her.

'Yes,' she admitted. 'Thank you. I intended using charcoal as usual, but in light like this I'd be mad not to try my hand at water-colour.'

'For that you'll need water, I suppose,' said James, resigned. 'Hand over a container and I'll get it for you from the burn down there.'

She handed him some plastic jars. 'You must be wishing I'd caught that train.'

James made no attempt to deny it as he disappeared down the ladder again with enviable agility. When he returned with the water he consulted his watch. 'Time I was off. When do you want me to come back for you?'

Flora tore her eyes from the view with effort. 'Oh, up to you,' she said absently. 'Whatever time's convenient.'

James gave her several concise instructions about safety, made sure she had all she needed, then swung himself down over the top of the ladder with a brief farewell and left her alone with her view. Flora was so absorbed in wetting paper and taping it to her easel to dry that she barely noticed him go. Their quarrel, her decision to leave, everything was forgotten in her driving urge to record the scene below with at least a small fraction of the skill her aunt had brought to other views of the loch. This particular bird's-eye view was missing from the water-colours at Inch Cottage for the simple reason that Genista Lyon had suffered from vertigo. The climb to the top of the watchtower would have been one of the rare defeats the artist encountered during her unconventional life.

The moment the paper had dried, smooth and taut as a drum, Flora laid her first background wash then worked with absolute concentration all morning. The only interruption came when it dawned on her that with no bathroom on hand she was forced to climb down the tower and seek a discreet clump of bushes outside. With no one to steady the ladder her descent was a far more hair-raising affair than before, and by the time she was safely back at her vantage-point in the tower Flora felt tired. She sat on the floor with her back to the wall, panting and hot, then to her dismay she heard the familiar drone of the Land Rover, heralding James's return. She sighed, frustrated, in no mood to go back to Inch Cottage just yet.

But James, she found, hadn't come to collect her. He appeared at the top of the ladder with a rucksack slung over his shoulders.

'I thought you'd like some lunch,' he announced as he crossed to join her.

Flora stared at him, astonished. 'Lunch? I thought you'd come to blow the whistle.'

He shook his head. 'As far as I'm concerned you can stay here as long as you like while the light lasts. But not without food. Which,' he added, eyeing her, 'I intend to share with you. I've no time to return to Ardlochan to lunch alone.' And, letting himself down beside her on the grimy, splintered boards, he produced a giant container of sandwiches, an insulated flask of coffee, a bag of apples and a tin containing half a fruit cake. Then with the air of a conjurer James unbuckled another pocket on the rucksack and produced a polythene bag containing a soapy washcloth and a towel. 'For your hands,' he announced smugly.

Flora thanked him politely, dealt with her paint-stained hands, then fell on the sandwiches, which, James informed her, he had made himself from the roast beef left over from dinner the night before. Since he'd added salad greens and chives and provided a pot of mustard to go with them, Flora accepted them in the spirit they were offered, generous with her praise.

'No Agnes today?' she said indistinctly.

James shook his head. 'She came first thing to tidy up, but she was so worried about her father, I sent her packing. Old Donald's need is greater than mine. To be honest I'm not averse to a spell of peace and quiet in the house while Mother's in Edinburgh.'

Flora smiled, waving a hand about her. 'There's no shortage of peace up here!'

'How are you getting on?'

'Faster than I'd expected. The air's warm today so the washes are drying fast.' Her eyes clouded. 'Not that I'll be able to finish it, of course——'

'Why not?'

'Because I'm leaving tomorrow.'

There was silence for a moment. 'Do you have to, Flora?' said James eventually. He turned to look at her. 'There'll be no repeat performance of last night's episode, I assure you. So why not stay on for a while? At least long enough to finish your painting.'

She popped the last of her sandwich in her mouth and munched pensively. 'I suppose I could.'

'Weather like this doesn't happen every day at Ardlochan,' he pointed out. 'It seems a sin to waste it.'

Flora thought for a while longer, then nodded. 'All right, I'll stay. But only if you'll provide me with some fresh milk. I poured all mine down the sink this morning before I left.'

James promised her she could stock up with whatever provisions she liked from Ardlochan, then got up to go, insisting that the fruit cake and most of the coffee were left for Flora to dispose of later.

'If you're sensible you'll stop for a break now and then,' he said.

'I have to occasionally for drying-out purposes,' she assured him, crunching on an apple. 'Thank you for lunch, James. I had no idea I was so hungry.'

'Did you have any breakfast?'

'Only coffee. I was too angry to eat anything.' She leaned back against the wall, clasping her hands loosely round her knees as she glanced sideways at him. 'For very obvious reasons.'

His mouth tightened. 'I can't keep on apologising.'

'I don't expect you to. Anyway, I suppose I was partly to blame. I should have stopped things getting out of hand sooner——' She hesitated, eyeing him warily. 'But, as must also have been obvious, you took me by surprise.'

'That much I'd worked out for myself,' he said drily.

On impulse Flora leaned over and offered him her hand. 'Can't we just be friends?'

He shook it formally, then tugged on it slightly. Flora snatched it away and smiled mockingly. 'What a jumpy creature you are, to be sure. I was only going to pull you to your feet. Fear not, fair maiden. I shan't throw you on the floor and try to have my wicked way again.'

'That's a relief,' she said tartly. 'I'm not partial to splinters.'

James chuckled as he sprang to his feet. 'Time I was off.'

'Could you fetch more water first, please?'

When James returned with her pots Flora thanked him politely enough, but with an air of distraction he recognised, with a wry twist to his mouth, as a hint to take himself off to leave her in peace.

Apart from another necessary trip to ground level during the afternoon Flora worked steadily without interruption. When James came at last to collect her she was surprised the time had passed so swiftly.

'Could I leave everything here?' she asked, yawning.

'Of course. Am I allowed to look at your progress so far?'

'No! Not until it's finished.' Flora tidied her things together neatly, then surprised James by disdaining his help to climb down the ladder.

'You're very agile all of a sudden,' he remarked as she followed him down at speed.

'Practice,' she said briefly. 'It's easier now I've done it a couple of times.'

'I told you to stay up there,' he said sternly.

Flora chuckled as they emerged into the evening sunshine. 'I've been up there since early this morning, James. I had to come down now and again, for very obvious reasons!'

To her amusement he looked discomfited.

'Sorry! I never gave a thought to—to that sort of thing.'

'Neither did I until the need became imperative!'

'What shall we do about eating tonight?' he asked, as he handed her up into the Land Rover.

Flora looked down at her hands. 'We?'

'Yes,' he said firmly. 'You're on your own, so am I. I vote we join forces. We could seek out more sophisticated flesh-pots tonight, if you like.'

'I'm too tired for that kind of thing,' she said quickly, then in a belated attempt at appreciation, 'If you've got something I can cook I'll make supper at Inch Cottage——' She stopped short, flushing.

'Flora,' he said patiently. 'Read my lips. I won't repeat my mistake. You have my word. So come and raid my kitchen, wait for me to have a bath, then I'll drive you back and give you a hand with the meal. I'll even bring the dogs to act as chaperons, if you like.'

After its inauspicious start the day improved enormously for Flora as it went on. After a swift shower when she got home while James saw to the drinks the evening was more of a success than she would have believed possible after the débâcle of the night before. Perhaps the secret of its success was because James had given her no time alone to regret her capitulation. Nor was there the least hint of hostility or sexual tension between them as she prepared a meal. James Cameron seemed determined to prove he was content merely to be in her company as they ate without fuss at the kitchen table, the retrievers lolling at their feet.

Flora learned that James liked nothing better than standing thigh-high in the local river for hours fishing for trout or salmon, that he was a keen rugby follower who went as often as possible to cheer on Scotland at Murrayfield, and that until recently he'd done a great deal of mountain climbing.

'These days I don't have the time,' he said with regret. 'What kind of sport do you like, Flora?'

'My father was a keen cricketer, so I was brought up to be a fan. In fact,' she confessed, 'I like nothing better than sitting in front of the television watching test cricket all day long in summer when term ends. Otherwise I play tennis, enjoy watching Wimbledon, swim a bit in the pool at school. You know about the sketching, but I like music, too. Most kinds, but quite a lot of opera—another taste Aunt Jenny encouraged.'

He pulled a face. 'Not my kind of music, I'm afraid.'

'In fact,' said Flora, 'we don't really have much in common, do we?'

'Not on the face of it.' He leaned back in his chair, relaxed. 'Yet from the first I've felt there's common ground between us somewhere.'

'Perhaps we met in the past in some other incarnation,' she said cheerfully.

James sat bolt upright, clapping a hand to his forehead. 'Talking of things past, Agnes asked me to give you a message from Jean, but our action-packed day sent it straight out of my head!'

'What did Jean say?'

'She's now the grandmother of a bouncing baby boy, by the way, but the message was to ask you to explore the attic. You'll find a trunk and a box which belonged to your aunt. Jean wondered if you'd take them with you when you went.'

'On the *train*?'

'I can always send them by carrier.' James jumped to his feet. 'Come on, let's explore.'

Flora followed him upstairs eagerly. 'I've been dying to explore up there, but I wasn't brave enough. I wasn't sure how far the electricity reached and I didn't care for the idea with only a candle for company.'

James grinned as he pressed a switch to light up a narrow stairway at the end of the upper hall. 'Don't tell me you were scared, Flora!'

'I certainly was. I didn't fancy meeting the ghost of Charles Edward Cameron.'

James laughed. 'He'd have been charm itself to a beautiful intruder like you.'

In actual fact the attic was no cobwebby hideaway full of ghosts, as Flora had expected, but merely a top floor with a corridor and a few small rooms leading off it. All of them were clean as a pin, and still furnished with the basic pieces provided for the servants who had once occupied them. A pair of larger rooms at the end were used for storage, where the expected bric-a-brac of a bygone age was stacked together in such order that it was no great task to find the large packing-case and trunk which Jean MacPhail had labelled very clearly with Genista Lyon's name. Flora had no eyes for discarded pieces of furniture and pictures, an elderly sewing machine and a tailor's dummy, stuffed birds in glass cases, a few antlered heads with staring, bored eyes. All her attention was centred on the packing-case.

'Shall I open it for you?' said James.

She nodded eagerly, almost dancing with impatience as he prised up the lid. James burrowed under layers of straw and newspaper, then turned to look back at Flora.

'There are two canvases in here, I think, much larger than any of the water-colours downstairs.'

Flora's eyes glittered with excitement. 'Let's get them out, then!'

The canvases had been very carefully packed. James propped them against the crate to let Flora remove the wrappings, then gave a startled exclamation as the first picture emerged.

'*Dia*!' he said, in a choked voice.

They both stared in silence at the study in oil of a commanding man in full, conventional evening dress, the severe black and white a perfect foil for his thick blond hair and piercing grey eyes. He was standing before the fireplace in the formal drawing-room of Inch Cottage, a smile playing at the corners of his mouth and an intimate gleam in his eyes for the artist who had reproduced his charisma with such skill.

CHAPTER SEVEN

'ALLOW me to present Charles Edward Cameron,' said James, letting out a deep breath.

Flora swept the portrait a curtsy. 'How do you do?' she said formally, then smiled, her eyes gleaming in excitement. 'No prizes for guessing the subject of the other one.'

She removed the wrappings with care and propped the second canvas alongside its companion, her throat tightening.

'Your aunt Jenny,' said James quietly.

Flora gazed in silence at the self-portrait of Genista then back at Charles Cameron. As far as she knew the canvases were the only oils in existence by Genista Lyon, yet both of them were triumphant testimonies to Aunt Jenny's skill. There was no doubt as to authenticity. The initials G.L. and the year 1937 were just discernible at the bottom right-hand corner of both portraits. The artist had been thirty-seven years old and at the height of her physical allure when she'd elected to paint herself in a clinging satin evening dress with her hair piled high on her head and a light in her eyes to match her lover's.

'You're like her, Flora,' said James slowly, 'but not as much as I'd imagined.'

'I don't hold a candle to her,' said Flora, sighing.

James gave her a look very different from the impersonal friendliness of the past couple of hours. 'You're mistaken,' he said flatly, then frowned. 'Did she never mention these?'

'No. Not a word. She never worked in oil.' Flora shook her head. 'I can't imagine why. She could have made a fortune painting portraits like these.'

'What will you do with them?'

'Do?'

'They're quite a size. Where will you hang them?'

She stared at him, eyebrows raised. 'James, the paintings are *your* property, not mine.'

'Miss Lyon left only the water-colours downstairs to me. She made no mention of these.' James looked down his nose with hauteur, suddenly very much the laird of Ardlochan. 'I've no intention of depriving you of what's rightfully yours.'

Flora bristled, her hackles erect in a flash. 'As I am by hanging on to Inch Cottage, you mean!'

'Since you mention it, yes.'

'I'm legally within my rights!'

His wide, flexible mouth tightened. 'Legally, yes, but morally you've no right at all to Inch Cottage, and you know it.'

Flora, who knew it perfectly well, stared at him defiantly. 'What I find so hard to understand is why you want it so badly when you already own a house and estate like Ardlochan. It smacks of greed to me, James Cameron.'

'It's not greed to want my own property returned to me.' His eyes hardened. 'And if it's greed we're discussing, are you free of it yourself where this place is concerned?'

Flora's chin lifted. 'That's entirely different.'

'I fail to see it.' He moved closer, his eyes boring down into hers. 'But since you're so curious you might as well know I've got plans for Inch Cottage—plans my grandfather approved years ago, when I was an idealistic youth bursting with ideas for the future of Ardlochan.'

'What sort of plans?' asked Flora, secretly rather moved.

James smiled sardonically. 'Since for the moment they're irrelevant there's no point in discussing them.' Then with an abruptness which caught her off balance he reverted to the impersonal friendliness of earlier on. 'Which brings me back to these canvases. What do you want done with them?'

Flora, sorely tempted to turn over Inch Cottage there and then, lock, stock and barrel bar the portrait of Genista, reminded herself in the nick of time that the gesture was meant to be her parting shot to James Cameron, the day she left Ardlochan for good.

'I think,' she said slowly, 'that the best thing is for you to take Charles Edward and I'll arrange to store Genista somewhere.'

James frowned. 'You're making me a gift of the portrait?'

'Yes, of course. Where else should a portrait of Charles Cameron hang, if not at Ardlochan?'

'It could be of value. It's not right for me to accept it as a gift,' said James stiffly.

'Oh, don't be so pigheaded,' she said impatiently. 'Look on it as recompense, if you like.'

'Recompense?'

'For all the trouble I've caused—one way and another.'

Their eyes met and held, and suddenly the sexual tension between them returned in full force, a tangible, living thing which throbbed in the very air between them in the silence of the attic.

'Perhaps——' Flora began, then cleared her throat and began again. 'Perhaps you'd be kind enough to put the canvases back.' She smiled ruefully. 'After looking at masterpieces like these I feel very depressed about my own artistic talents.'

'Unnecessary,' said James very softly, a nuance in his tone which raised the hairs on her neck. 'You possess undeniable talents of your own.'

She stiffened, her eyes suspicious, and he smiled blandly as he began re-wrapping the canvases.

'Shall I store them away here again for the time being?' he asked.

'Yes, please. Our attic at home isn't the five-star kind like this one.' She went over to the trunk. 'I wonder what's in here?' She slid back the hasps and lifted the lid to reveal a sea of silver paper, and underneath it some linen bags. A faint, elusive drift of jasmine rose from them. 'Whatever it is definitely belonged to Aunt Jenny,' she said, sighing. 'She used the same perfume all her life. She told me a friend gave it to her when she was young, and she never found one she liked better.'

'For "friend" read Charles Cameron, I suppose.' James secured the lid of the packing crate with care before he joined her to peer in the trunk. 'What's in the bags?'

'I imagine it's clothes.' Flora pulled the drawstring of the first bag to reveal a drift of amber chiffon, and drew out an evening gown with the dropped waist and floating panels of twenties high fashion. The second bag yielded a gown from the following decade, bias-cut from heavy pastel satin.

James looked at them in silence for a moment, frowning. 'Her favourites, I suppose. But did she wear them here, do you think, just to dine alone in state with my grandfather?'

Flora shook her head, examining them closely. 'Paris labels—I'll bet he bought these on their holidays abroad.'

His eyes narrowed. 'Abroad? But I thought they only saw each other on her annual visit up here.'

'Apparently not. That wasn't nearly enough for Charles Cameron almost from the start. He began to meet Genista in Paris or Rome or the South of France every Easter school holiday as well. Her water-colours weren't all of Scotland by any means!' In full command of herself by this time, Flora gave him a wicked little smile.

'The old devil! I knew he went on holiday alone every year, of course, but he had friends in Tuscany so it was assumed he went there.'

'He may well have done, but if he did he took Aunt Jenny with him.'

They looked at each other for a moment, then James laughed. 'What a man!'

Flora held up the satin gown against her thoughtfully. 'What colour would you say this is?'

'No idea. The light's too bad to tell. Why?'

'I think it's the dress in the portrait.' She put it back in its bag, then returned the chiffon gown to the trunk, smoothed the paper wrappings in place and closed the lid. 'I'd like to see this one by daylight. I'll take it down to their room.'

'Is that how you think of it?' asked James as he followed her down the narrow attic stair.

'Do you wonder?' Flora paused outside the bedroom door. 'It may sound fanciful, but I never feel alone in here. If you go on down you can pour yourself a drink while I hang the dress up.'

'I wasn't going to set foot across the threshold, believe me,' said James drily. 'I may make mistakes, but rarely the same one twice.'

'Good.' She smiled at him cheerfully. 'You'll find a bottle of Glenlivet in the parlour. I'd bought it for my father, but I can easily get another one in Fort William when I leave.'

When Flora went downstairs she curled up on the sofa with her modest dram of whisky, and began asking James about the Urquhart dance. 'If I do come I imagine evening dress is *de rigueur*?'

'Why? Is a suitable dress a problem?'

'Probably not.' She rolled the smooth spirit round her tongue. 'Not that it matters much. I don't suppose anyone looks at the women with you fellows strutting about in your finery.'

'Not a bit of it.' James grinned as he explained that the ladies wore tartan too, but in clan sashes over the shoulder, on the right for wives of clan chiefs and serving officers, otherwise over the left.

Flora nodded thoughtfully. 'It all sounds splendid—and too good an opportunity to miss, I suppose.'

'We made a bargain, remember,' he reminded her.

'I know. But I keep wondering why you want me to keep to it,' she said bluntly.

James regarded her in silence for a moment, shaking his head. 'Are you really so naïve, Flora?'

'What do you mean?'

He tossed back the rest of his whisky, then looked her in the eye. 'What man wouldn't want a beautiful woman like you for his partner? Isn't that reason enough?'

'No,' she said flatly. 'Because I'm—who I am, and very much in your way here, I can't accept your overtures at face value. Not that I don't find them attractive,' she added honestly. 'Because I do. I've enjoyed our evening together—most of it, anyway. But every now and then something creeps in to remind me that possibly this is part of your plan to get Inch Cottage back.'

'Is that what you thought I was doing last night?' he demanded, his jaw set. 'You really think I was trying to seduce you into giving up the tenancy?'

'Well, weren't you?' she retorted defiantly.

'No, I bloody well wasn't——' He stopped short, controlling his temper with effort. 'As I've said before, *ad nauseam*, last night was a mistake.' He breathed in deeply, then looked her in the eye. 'Listen, Flora Blair. I've a proposition to make. Because I had to make a bargain to keep you here for Catriona's dance I assume that once it's over you intend to leave. So for the short time remaining I suggest I take you to the tower each morning, fetch you back in the evening, which we then spend together. Here, Ardlochan or anywhere you choose.'

'Why?'

'Because that's what I want!'

Her eyes narrowed. 'And you always get what you want?'

'Without fail,' he said simply.

'You haven't asked if it's what I want,' she pointed out.

'It was merely a suggestion. Just tell me you don't care for the idea and the subject's closed.' He leaned back in his chair, apparently relaxed as Flora thought it over. If she said it was the last thing she wanted she'd be lying, as she— and James—well knew. And in a few days she'd be gone from here and she'd never see him again.

'If I don't agree,' she said slowly at last, 'will you forbid me access to the tower?'

'Very definitely.'

'Then I don't have much choice, do I?'

'None.'

Flora shrugged casually. 'Then agree I must, if only to get my painting finished. It's unlikely I'll get another chance.'

'Why?' he said instantly. 'Surely you'll make future visits to Inch Cottage?'

'Of course.' She smiled sweetly. 'But I might not be so lucky with the weather another time.'

James gave her a mocking smile and got to his feet. 'How right you are. It's time I went. Thank you for cooking dinner.'

'You provided the food.'

James looked down at her in silence for so long that Flora became restive.

'What now?' she demanded at last, her colour high.

'I was weighing up the cause and effect of a certain course of action,' he said musingly, and before she realised what he had in mind he pulled her up into his arms and kissed her very thoroughly. When he raised his head he was breathing hard. 'It was a risk worth taking,' he informed her, stepping back.

Flora pulled herself together, pushing a hand through her hair. 'Risk?' she said unevenly.

'That I might find you packed and ready to leave again in the morning.'

'Not this time! I told you, James, now I've started it I'm determined to finish my watercolour.'

'In that case I'll be over to collect you in the morning, bright and early. Be ready,' he added, strolling to the door.

'As long as you see me up the tower once I get there I could drive over to Ardlochan myself,' contradicted Flora, following him into the hall.

He gave her an indulgent smile. 'Talented you may be, but that you'd find impossible without a battery. See you in the morning.'

The settled, sunny days formed a pattern as the week wore on. Each morning James saw Flora and her belongings safely up the ladder to the top of the watchtower, and late each afternoon he returned to fetch her back to Ardlochan House or Inch Cottage for the evening.

James made no further mention of the tenancy, took good care to avoid his commando tactics of the first evening, but, rather to Flora's surprise, never suggested taking her out somewhere to dinner. Not that she minded. In various subtle ways James made it plain that all he expected was Flora's company, and, while she assured herself she was pleased, she secretly would have preferred a slightly less platonic approach. She suffered deep disappointment each night when James parted from her with no more than a nonchalant goodnight, more convinced than ever that he was up to some devious ploy, that he was merely biding his time before launching into phase two of his plan to charm her out of Inch Cottage. And all the time his company grew more addictive with each day, her pleasure in it heightened by the underlying sexual chemistry which lurked beneath the

banter like embers threatening to burst into
flame at the slightest provocation.

Flora knew she was in grave danger of falling
in love with James Cameron. Something about
his contained, negligent self-confidence held an
appeal stronger than anything possessed by any
other man she'd ever met. Including, she
thought remorsefully, Tom Harvey, who was
looking forward to joining her in France. She
wrote bright, chatty letters to him and to her
dismay found it hard to conjure up his face,
her inner eye monopolised by the dark, forceful
features of James Cameron. Flora found
thoughts of James beginning to encroach as she
painted, high up in the tower, her growing
predilection for his company adding a lustre to
life which showed in her work, adding an extra
dimension to her talent. Whatever fate had in
store in future, she thought, sighing, one look
at the paintings would always be enough to
transport her back in time to the here and now
of her first—and probably last—visit to
Ardlochan.

One golden day succeeded another, like glittering beads strung on a chain, until the eve of
the Urquhart dance arrived, and James was
very late coming to collect Flora. She was on
edge and impatient by the time he put in an
appearance, and found it hard to be civil when

she learned the reason for his delay was a visit from Catriona.

'I'm sorry, Flora.' He shrugged as he took her bag. 'She was in no hurry to go home—full of her dance and the dress she's bought for the occasion.'

'Oh, is it late? I didn't notice,' lied Flora, and started down the ladder at reckless speed, shaken by a violent pang of jealousy, as illuminating as it was unwelcome.

After Agnes MacPhail, now firmly back in charge at Ardlochan, had served them dinner that night, Flora looked at James quizzically as they sat on the terrace, admiring the sunset.

'Was Catriona disappointed to learn I was still here, by the way?'

James shrugged. 'I didn't ask her. If she was it makes no difference. She doesn't dictate to me in any way.'

'Nor does anyone else, I suppose,' said Flora, shaking her head. 'You're much too used to getting your own way. Laird of Ardlochan and all that. Very feudal.'

'Nothing feudal about me, lassie! I work as hard as any man on the estate.'

'Good for you.' She yawned suddenly. 'If you work that hard you must be tired, like me. If I'm to be in any shape for Catriona's dance tomorrow I'd better be off in a minute.' To her disappointment James made no move to dissuade her.

'Will you be painting tomorrow?' he asked as they strolled to the car.

'I'd better not. I really must go into Fort William and buy some sort of gift for the birthday girl.'

'She won't expect one.'

'Nevertheless I shall make the gesture—if only to sweeten the pill of my presence!' Flora hesitated, then said casually, 'Catriona seems more than a touch possessive where you're concerned, James.'

'We've known each other all our lives,' he said, making no effort to deny it. 'After she got married I didn't see much of her for a while, but lately——'

'Married?' Flora stared in surprise. 'But she was introduced to me as an Urquhart.'

James nodded. 'Catriona married a distant cousin, years older, with pots of money. He died last year.'

'So she's not only a beautiful widow, but a wealthy one!'

'Very. Not that——' He glanced up as the telephone rang inside the house. 'Back in a minute.'

When he returned he was laughing. 'That, would you believe, was Mistress Isobel

Cameron. She's decided to return home for the dance after all and is, as we speak, drinking coffee at the Alexandra Hotel in Fort William, waiting for me to pick her up. Apparently she rang earlier to say she was coming but no one was in.'

Flora felt a sharp secret pang of regret. Much as she liked his mother, Mrs Cameron's return signalled the end of her interlude with James. The paintings were almost finished; soon there would be no excuse at all to linger at Ardlochan. Already Lucy Blair was asking curious questions in her letters about her daughter's protracted stay at Inch Cottage. It was quite definitely time to go. And Flora found she hated the very thought of it.

She was so abstracted during the journey back to Inch Cottage that James frowned as he saw her to the door.

'Is there something wrong, Flora?'

She shook her head, smiling. 'No, of course not. I'm just tired.'

James leaned in the open doorway, his eyes inscrutable. 'Would it reawaken all your original suspicions if I told you how much I regret my mother's interruption of our little idyll?'

'Idyll?'

'What else would you call these past few days? Pure, uncomplicated enjoyment of each other's company. Something new to me with a woman. There was only one thing lacking to make it perfect,' he added softly. 'Shared nights as well as days.'

Flora's chin lifted. 'That was never remotely possible, so it's just as well it's time for me to go. Once the party's over I'll pack up my paints and take myself off, out of harm's way. Out of Catriona's way, too,' she added sweetly.

James stared at her in silence for a moment, then took her by the shoulders and kissed her with a force and hunger which put an abrupt end to his self-restraint of the past week. When he raised his head at last they stared at each other in silence, both of them breathing as if they'd run all the way from Ardlochan. He dropped his hands and stood back. 'Does my fall from grace mean I've lost a partner for to-morrow night?'

Flora blinked, dazed, and pulled herself together. 'No. I promised I'd come, so I will.' She hesitated. 'In fact I thought you might care to bring your mother here for a drink before we go.'

James smiled, surprised. 'Mother will like that very much. So will I,' he added deliberately. His eyes fell to her mouth, making her retreat a little, and he laughed softly. 'Don't worry. I shan't push my luck. Until tomorrow, then, Flora. Sweet dreams.'

Flora, sure she would never achieve enough sleep to dream after James's kiss, spent a surprisingly restful night, and woke feeling very much better for it. Over the past few days her intense concentration on her work, coupled with the almost constant excitement she felt in James's presence, had been a double drain on her energies. After the best night's sleep she'd had for a week or so she felt recharged and full of unexpected enthusiasm for Catriona's dance, mainly, as she very well knew, because James was taking her there. And when he brought her home, decided Flora over breakfast, she'd tell him at long last that she'd never had the least intention of hanging on to Inch Cottage.

After days isolated at the top of a ruin Flora enjoyed her browse round the shops in Fort William. The problem of Catriona's present took some time to solve, but at last Flora opted for safety with an exquisite Caithness crystal paperweight which she hoped would strike the right impersonal note. She was less successful in finding shoes to wear to the party, and the moment she was back at Inch Cottage went up to the attic, hoping her hunch was correct. With care Flora lifted out the contents of the trunk, one by one, and at the bottom struck oil. Inside a cardboard box she found two pairs of tissue-wrapped satin slippers, one pair amber, with double straps and rhinestone buttons, the other in the exact shade of the dress in the portrait.

Flora crossed her fingers as she tried on the pale satin slippers, cock-a-hoop to find that, though a trifle loose, they were definitely wearable.

'Well done, Cinderella,' she crowed. 'You *shall* go to the ball.'

She smiled wickedly as she pictured James's reaction when he saw her in the dress. The moment she'd laid eyes on it Flora had known exactly what to wear to Catriona Urquhart's dance. The inspired simplicity of Aunt Jenny's gown would be the perfect foil for the vivid finery of the menfolk.

A minute examination of the dress by daylight had shown no signs of deterioration in the heavy satin. The delicate tinge of blush pink was as subtle and fresh as the tints in the portrait. Understated as a slip, the bias-cut gown clung to Flora's breasts and slithered over her hips with such flattery that she felt confident of its suitability for the occasion.

With no jewelry to rival the pearls worn by Genista Lyon in the portrait Flora kept to a slender gold bracelet as her only ornament. She stood in the hall when she was ready, surveying herself critically in the mirror as she administered the final touches to her hair, which hung loose in gleaming ripples to her shoulders. Tonight, she knew without doubt, she looked as good as she'd ever looked in her life.

Flora went into the parlour to make sure glasses were in readiness, along with the dry sherry and salted nuts and biscuits she'd bought that morning. She smiled as the heavy satin flowed sensuously against her legs with every movement. What pleasure Genista Lyon must have taken in decking herself out like this for her lover. Which, Flora reminded herself wryly, was not so far from what she was doing herself right this minute. Except that James Cameron was not her lover. Nor would it be wise to consider the possibility, alluring though it might be.

When she heard James's car, prompt as always to the promised minute, Flora hurried to open the door wide in welcome to her guests. Isobel Cameron, majestic in dark green silk embellished with the Cameron green and red tartan sash over her shoulder, her magnificent pearls much in evidence, smiled warmly in greeting.

Flora held out her hand. 'Good evening, Mrs Cameron. Do come in.'

'Last night,' said James forcibly, 'was a mistake on my part—a human, stupid male mistake.'

'Including the insults?' she demanded hotly.

His face set. 'I'm sorry. I apologise for what I said. It's my bloody Cameron temper. I just had to lash out. But I was lying. I've never pretended bogus feelings to get a woman to bed, and certainly not with you. I came on a damn sight too strong, I know, Flora. But it was nothing to do with that bloody bedroom, or my grandfather, or anything other than the fact that you're an alluring, desirable woman, and I wanted to make love to you.'

She stared at him stonily. 'A pity you were so convincing with your parting shot.'

James ground his teeth. 'Flora, don't you know the first thing about men? I wanted you so much I was out of control. And for a while you weren't indifferent yourself. Then suddenly full stop. You slammed on the brakes. I was frustrated, furious, and said the first thing that came into my head out of sheer bloody-mindedness.' He breathed in deeply. 'If you'd had a phone I'd have rung you the minute I got home. But the only way I could have apologised was to drive back last night. I wasn't idiot enough to try that, so I left it until this morning. Almost too late,' he added, eyeing the luggage.

'My dear, how nice that you could stay for Catriona's dance.' Mrs Cameron looked Flora up and down. 'And how very lovely you look. Doesn't she, James?'

James, unusually, had nothing to say. Resplendent himself in the finery of his first dramatic appearance at Inch Cottage, he was staring at Flora as though he'd never seen her before.

His mother looked at him askance. 'You look as though you'd seen a ghost, James.'

Flora laughed, and led the way into the parlour. 'In a way he has.' She explained about the portrait. 'At first I meant to refuse Ewen's invitation, mostly because I had nothing formal to wear. Then your Agnes passed on a message from Jean about some things in the attic, and— hey presto!—Cinderella was able to go to the ball.'

Mrs Cameron accepted a glass of sherry, fascinated to discover that Flora was wearing a dress made more than fifty years before.

'It's very beautiful,' she said, then looked about her with interest. 'And so is this room. It must be years since I was last here. Are those the water-colours you've inherited, James?'

But James wasn't listening. His entire attention was centred on Flora as she handed him a glass of whisky. 'You look ravishing, as you well know,' he said in an undertone.

She smiled radiantly. 'I thought I'd surprise you.'

'You have!'

Flora turned away, aware that his mother was surveying them with interest. 'Did you enjoy your stay in Edinburgh, Mrs Cameron?'

'Very much.' Mrs Cameron's eyes twinkled. 'I gather you've been making good use of the time since I left.'

Flora nodded fervently. 'I certainly have. The weather's been so perfect I've actually done *two* water-colours of the view from the watchtower. Another hour's work should see the second one finished.'

'Flora's become adept at shinning up that ladder.' James smiled with irony. 'It's hard to associate the paint-stained artist with the movie-star vision of tonight.'

'Of course!' exclaimed his mother. 'That's it, exactly. Actresses like Carole Lombard and Madeleine Carroll made that kind of dress fashionable before the war.'

'My mother's mad on old black and white films,' James said, resigned.

'Really, Mrs Cameron?' Flora beamed. 'So am I. That's why the dress appealed so much.

I just love those sophisticated thirties comedies!'

The two women plunged into an animated discussion about their favourites, so absorbed that James was forced to interrupt at last.

'We've a long drive ahead of us so let's away, Mother, and show Flora how to enjoy herself in true Highland style.'

CHAPTER EIGHT

DUE to Mrs Cameron's dislike of speed the party from Ardlochan arrived rather late at Strathroy, the home of the Urquharts. Lights were already blazing along an impressive terrace and in every window of a house totally unlike the traditional Scottish charm of Ardlochan. Strathroy was a Georgian mansion which would have looked at home almost anywhere in Britain. Music and laughter met them in a blast as James gave his keys into the keeping of a young man who promised to treat the precious vehicle with the respect it deserved.

'Right, then, ladies,' said James, offering an arm to each of his charges. 'Time to face the music.'

The senior Urquharts were waiting to welcome them in an octagonal hall painted deep coral-red, with white alcoves full of costly porcelain. Against a background of stamping feet and skirling cries from the ballroom, where an enthusiastic band was thumping out the rhythm of an eightsome reel, there were kisses and handshakes for Isobel and James Cameron, a more formal welcome for Flora. A shattering roll of drums signalled the end of the reel and right on cue Ewen Urquhart came hurrying into the hall, his square face flushed with pleasure at the sight of Flora. Behind him swept Catriona in beaded white lace, with the dark green and blue tartan sash of her clan over her shoulder. Magnificent sapphires in her ears, her hair like black satin, she fairly radiated triumph and pleasure as she welcomed James and his mother, exclaiming over their gifts with voluble delight which faded abruptly as she turned to Flora.

'How nice you could stay for my party after all,' she said, her tone conveying the exact opposite.

'Not at all. I wouldn't have missed it for the world,' countered Flora, smiling serenely as she held out her beribboned package. 'Happy birthday.'

Catriona took it as though the package contained something noisome. She unwrapped the exquisite glass bauble, thanked Flora carelessly, then thrust the paperweight on a shelf in one of the recesses and seized James by the arm as the band struck a chord in the ballroom.

'Do come on, James—time for the "Dashing White Sergeant".' She paused for a moment, looking over her shoulder. 'I don't suppose you're familiar with this sort of thing, Miss Blair. Never mind. Ewen, look after her, will you?' Catriona tugged impatiently at James, who gave Flora a wry look as he went, perforce, to join the reel with his hostess.

'I'd be honoured to teach you,' offered Ewen eagerly, but Mrs Cameron laughed.

'No need, laddie. On the way over here Flora told me she's done this kind of thing before.'

'I'm no expert,' Flora said hastily, 'But I think I can manage not to tread all over you.'

Ewen informed her with fervour that he didn't mind in the least if she did, and bore her off into the ballroom. Flora barely had time for an awed stare at flower-wreathed pillars and barrel-vaulted ceiling before she was drawn into an eightsome with three girls in voluminous white dresses and the inevitable sashes, two army officers in scarlet mess jackets, and a tall man in black jacket, white bow-tie and a kilt in the distinctive orange and black Drummond tartan. With no time for formal introductions, Flora was immediately circling and swinging, linking arms and changing partners with the best of them as she kept time to the beat of music supplied by drums, accordion and a trio of very enthusiastic fiddles. Now and again she caught sight of James's dark head above the others, but in the main found she was enjoying herself so much that for the time being she was content to cede Catriona her little victory. Tonight might be Catriona Urquhart's birthday celebration, thought Flora, smiling brilliantly at Ewen, but at the same time it was a very special occasion for Flora Blair, too. This was her farewell fling before she went back where she belonged, and nothing, she was determined, would be allowed to mar her enjoyment.

Flushed and laughing when a roll of drums brought the reel to an end, Flora was introduced to her fellow dancers before the army officers took their ladies in search of a drink. Alasdair Cargill, the civilian, assured her he was an old friend of James Cameron, and with his sister Janet who'd partnered him lingered to chat until James joined them, with Catriona in tow.

James wrung his friend's hand, kissed Janet, then turned to Flora. 'How did you cope, Flora?' he asked, as a waiter served them with champagne. 'You seemed to be acquitting yourself remarkably well.'

'No coping about it,' said Ewen emphatically. 'She's an expert.'

'Well, well,' said Catriona, eyes glittering. 'What a lady of talent you are, Miss Blair.'

Flora smiled cheerfully. 'I lend a hand with games at school. Scottish dancing is part of the curriculum.' She turned to James. 'Where's your mother?'

'Gossiping with old friends in the card-room across the hall. She'll join us for supper.' He glanced up as the band played a chord. 'Right, we're off again.'

'My favourite, the "Duke of Perth",' said Alasdair, and, before James could make a move, bowed to Flora. 'May I, Miss Blair?'

In the ballroom others surged towards them to make a sixteensome, and it was suppertime before a rather breathless Flora was granted any private conversation with James. When the meal was announced Catriona, obliged as hostess to circulate among her guests, glared impotently as James took Flora to join his mother. Mrs Cameron, however, was happy to be left with a party of friends for supper, and once she was satisfied Flora was enjoying herself waved her off with James. In the dining-room James swiftly filled two plates with a selection of delicacies, turned a blind eye to hands beckoning them to various tables and suggested they go outside on the terrace.

'If we double back through the hall no one will guess where we're heading,' he said into her ear.

Not at all sure she should be following so obediently where James led, Flora hurried with him through the octagonal extravagance of the hall, laughing as they emerged on to the terrace, where subdued lighting fell on urns full of flowers nurtured to the peak of perfection for this special night, but otherwise very satisfactorily deserted.

With the skill of a man familiar with his terrain James led her to a remote, shadowy corner, and spread his handkerchief on the stone balustrade for Flora to sit down.

'Should we really be out here?' she asked breathlessly, as he handed her a plate.

James shrugged, then leaned against the wall above her to eat his own meal. 'Why not? I wanted you to myself for a while, and this seemed the best way to achieve it. Why? Do you object?'

'No,' said Flora honestly, only too happy to be alone with James. Hungry after her exertions, she paid full attention to her supper while he asked her opinion of her first taste of Highland hospitality.

'Marvellous. And great fun.' She smiled up at him. 'At least at a dance like this it doesn't matter about partners. Everyone's thrown in together.'

'You wouldn't lack partners at any dance.' James took her plate and set it aside with his. 'I gather that for the less energetic there's some kind of nightclub affair later down in the cellar.'

'The Urquharts are lavish with their hospitality!'

'No lack of money at Strathroy. Catriona's not exactly on the breadline either.'

Flora looked out across the shadowy, formal gardens. 'It must be pleasant to be rich as well as beautiful.'

'Just beautiful like you is more than enough.'

Their eyes met, and suddenly the tension was back. They stared at each other in silence, the pull between them so strong that Flora forgot her surroundings and yielded to the impulse which drew her to her feet and into James's outstretched arms. She trembled as she felt his heart thundering against her own, then he held her away and looked down at her, his eyes glittering.

'As must be all too obvious,' he said, a note in his voice which turned her bones to water, 'all I can think of at this moment is how much I want to kiss you.' His breathing accelerated as she moved nearer. 'But if I do I might not stop.'

Flora said nothing, her eyes so eloquent that James Cameron drew in a sharp breath then kissed her hard, his arms tightening around her, his square silver cuff buttons biting into her bare back. Flora, oblivious to the pain, responded so whole-heartedly that it was a long time before he raised his head to look into her face. He brushed back a lock of her hair with a possessive hand. 'Why didn't this happen before, when we had privacy and time to ourselves, Flora Blair?'

She smiled, her eyes luminous. 'Because tonight everything's different.'

His answering smile was wry. 'You're confident that here, with Ewen and company close at hand, I won't get out of hand.'

Flora shook her head. 'No, that's not the reason at all.' She smoothed a hand down her dress. 'Don't laugh, but somehow there's a kind of magic about tonight, probably because you're in your kilt, and I'm wearing Aunt Jenny's gown. It's the Cinderella factor. I wouldn't be surprised if my satin changed to rags at midnight!'

'If you're Cinderella, do I take it I'm cast for the prince?' His arm tightened round her waist.

'Ah, yes. A very *bonny* prince——' Her remaining words were lost against his mouth, and a long, breathless interval passed before she steeled herself to push gently at his restraining arms.

'Time we went back, James.' She smiled up at him, her regret plain in her eyes for him to see.

He nodded, crushing her hand in his. 'I suppose you're right. Ewen's probably setting up a search party by this time.'

'Not to mention Catriona,' said Flora, smoothing her hair, then bit her lip. 'Talk of the devil—or do I mean Nemesis?'

James choked back a laugh as Catriona swept out on to the terrace with Ewen at her heels.

'So this is where you are!' said their hostess accusingly.

'We decided to eat our supper out here in company with the stars,' said James suavely. 'We were just coming in search of you.'

'And not before time. There are masses of people in there wanting to talk to you,' she snapped. 'Ewen! Take care of Miss Blair for a while.'

James stiffened, but Flora touched his hand fleetingly and smiled. 'I'll enjoy that. Perhaps you'll find some coffee for me, Ewen.'

Nothing loth, Ewen took her off to the dining-room and installed her at a small table with the Cargills, where Flora spent an agreeable few minutes in their company before the band struck up again in the ballroom, calling the dancers back to the fray.

With her colour high and her eyes sparkling, the blood singing through her veins after James's lovemaking, Flora left him to Catriona for a while as she became part of the whirling colour and regimented rhythm, her feet light as she stepped and twirled and clapped to the beat of the music. It was the best part of an hour before James managed to take her from the floor to say goodnight to Mrs Cameron, who, surprisingly, was on the point of departure.

'I'm going to stay the night near by with Mary and Hector Elliott,' she informed them. 'It's long past my bedtime. Hector will drive me home in the morning, so you two can stay as long as you like.' She patted Flora's cheek. 'See you soon, my dear.'

James waved the Elliotts' car out of sight, unfastened his sporran and tossed it to the man in charge of the parking. 'Keep that safe for me, Andy.' He caught Flora by the hand. 'Right. No more tribal mayhem. Let's away down to the cellar. At least there I'll have the perfect excuse to hold you in my arms for a while.'

The cellar was actually a small basement room, done out with dark drapes and a minimum of light as the disc jockey, in tune with the dancers' need for respite, played the slowest, moodiest music in his collection for the couples welded together in the gloom.

As James took Flora in his arms the heat from his body seared through the heavy satin of her dress, and her blood leapt in response as he pulled her closer. Not even pretending to move from the spot, they swayed together in time to the slow, inflammatory beat, and after a while James touched his lips to the hollow below her ear, sending a shiver down her spine.

'We're leaving. Now.' He took her hand in a bone-cracking grip and led her through the dancers and up the stairs to the hall.

'We must thank our hostess,' said Flora huskily, not daring to meet his eyes.

'Where's your mother?' asked Catriona sharply when they sought her out.

'She went off earlier with the Elliotts,' said James. 'She asked me to convey her thanks for a splendid evening.'

Ewen, meanwhile, was making a hesitant attempt to ask Flora for a further meeting. 'Dinner, a cinema, anything you like,' he said eagerly.

She explained that her stay was unlikely to last long enough. 'But thank you for asking. Perhaps another time. And thank you for inviting me tonight.' Flora turned to Catriona. 'My thanks to you also, Mrs Urquhart.'

'Don't mention it,' said Catriona coldly. 'How lucky you were able to fit it in before you leave.'

'No luck about it. I persuaded her.' James took Flora by the hand, ignoring the outrage in Catriona's eyes. 'Let's be on our way, then. Goodnight to you both, and our thanks again for a splendid party.'

There was silence in the car for a while as James made for home at twice the speed of the journey with his mother. 'Are you nervous?' he asked after a while. 'I kept to one glass of champagne, I promise.'

'Not in the least.' She stretched like a cat, feeling deliriously happy now they were alone together. 'You know, James, I had grave doubts about turning up tonight, yet I had a wonderful time.'

'So I noticed,' he said drily. 'You rather stole Catriona's thunder. I overheard one or two comments about your dress and clever lack of jewels.'

'Nothing clever about it,' said Flora, amused. 'I don't have any jewels. In any case,' she added, 'once I put the dress on it seemed best to let it speak for itself.'

He touched long fingers to her satin-clad knee for an instant. 'Which it did, loud and clear—to me, anyway, as must be perfectly obvious.'

They exchanged an unsmiling look, then James returned his concentration to the road and Flora settled lower in her seat with a sigh.

'What a fabulously beautiful night. I've never seen such stars. You must have a special brand up here in Scotland.'

'Arranged specially for the occasion, to please you!'

The roads were quiet as they made for Ardlochan. They could have been the only people in the world awake as they sped through the starlit darkness, and in miraculously short time James turned up the track to Inch Cottage and Flora was home.

He took the key from her silently, and unlocked the door, then followed her into the hall and closed the door behind him. They both stood very still, Flora at the foot of the stairs in her gleaming dress, James with his back to the door, outrageously attractive in his Highland finery.

'This takes me back to our first meeting,' said Flora unevenly, her quickened breathing very evident to the eyes of the man watching her so intently. 'You materialised out of the night like the Bonny Prince himself.'

'You were no greater surprise, with your hair in a rope down your back and that ridiculous candlestick.' James moved an inch or two in her direction, his eyes locked with hers. 'Are your feelings warmer towards me tonight, *mo cridhe*?'

The endearment reduced Flora's crumbling defences to nothing. When she nodded wordlessly James closed the space between them with such triumphant certainty that she melted against him, shivering with excitement as his hands slid down her ribs and over the satin-covered curve of her hips. Kissing her deeply, hungrily, he moved his fingers up her spine and round her ribcage, lingering over their journey to the breasts which thrust against her dress, their nipples pointing and erect in anticipation of his touch. She stiffened at the exquisite sorcery of his fingertips, and moaned softly, deeply in her throat, locking her arms about his neck in sudden, frantic response. James raised his head to look deep in her eyes, his own darkening until the pupils looked like onyx discs set in rims of silver. Suddenly she buried her face against his shoulder and he lifted her into his arms.

'This time...' he began against her hair.

'This time,' she said very deliberately, raising her head to look at him, 'will be different.'

James kissed her hard, then carried her up the stairs and set her on her feet, closing the door behind him as Flora turned on the lamps. They moved together involuntarily, and stood, almost touching, at the foot of the bed, both of them breathing raggedly as the sensual charm of the room added fuel to the fire beginning to consume them both. Flora pushed back a lock of bright, dishevelled hair, her eyes luminous with invitation, and James's arms shot out to crush her to him. He kissed her eyes and her nose and her parted, eager mouth.

'Tell me you want me,' he commanded, his arms tightening cruelly.

Flora stiffened involuntarily, then melted against him, standing on tiptoe to rub her cheek against his. 'I thought I had,' she whispered.

James breathed in sharply and slid the satin straps from her shoulders, undressing her swiftly, with an expertise she barely had time to register before they were together in the great, wide bed, their finery discarded and their bodies together in such glorious, naked contact that for a while it was enough. But soon she stirred restlessly, and James laughed deep in his throat as he began to make love to her with slow subtlety, his caresses gentle at first, then increasing gradually and inexorably, arousing a response in Flora which astonished her with its intensity.

His lips and hands seemed possessed of a very personal, individual magic he wielded like a sorcerer, until Flora, at the mercy of her own senses, had to bite her lip to prevent herself begging him to end the exquisite torture in the only way possible to bring her relief.

When he raised his head to look deep into her heavy, dazed eyes as she lay staring up at him uncomprehendingly as he smiled and smoothed back her damp, tumbled hair.

'There's still time to say no,' he said unbelievably, and her eyes darkened, the colour rushing to her cheeks.

'You know very well I don't want to,' she said fiercely, and turned her head away, but he caught her chin in his hand and turned her face back to his.

'Then tell me what you do want, *mo cridhe*.'

Flora, her senses roused to fever pitch, felt tears well into her eyes and then James was licking them away, and kissing her mutinous mouth, and there was no need to tell him anything, as suddenly her tears were dry and her eyes open wide in wonder as he took possession of her at last. She gave a choked gasp of rapture as he began to move, slowly at first, then faster as her body responded. Together they achieved unison so quickly that the rhythm bore them inexorably towards the goal they reached within seconds of each other as wave after throbbing wave of heat and fulfilment broke over them, leaving them breathless and elated in the aftermath of the passion which had been building between them almost from the moment of their first meeting.

For a long, recuperative interval they lay still in each other's arms, until Flora stirred at last to find James gazing down at her. The look in his eyes was so explicit that her heart hammered as he began to kiss her, over and over again, his tongue importunate as his hands smoothed her hair and stroked her face then moved lower to caress her breasts, lingering and teasing with caresses which sent streaks of fire down to that part of her which still pulsed for him. He swung his hard, athletic body over hers, and, hardly able to believe this was happening to her, Flora clutched at his shoulders, gasping, and abandoned herself to magic even more powerful than the first time.

It was much later when Flora, in dressing-gown, and James, in carelessly draped bath-towel, went down to the kitchen together to raid the refrigerator. They went back up to bed to picnic, stifling their laughter as they stole up the stairs.

'Silly really. We don't need to be quiet. Aunt Jenny would approve,' said Flora, sitting cross-legged on the rumpled bed. James tossed a pillow against the brass foot-rail and leaned against it to watch her as she ate.

'So would he,' said James, waving a hand towards the drawing of his grandfather.

'We should have turned him to the wall,' said Flora, giggling.

'I doubt he was shocked!'

Flora thrust back her tangled hair thoughtfully as she munched on her sandwich. 'Do you suppose they made snacks in the middle of the night?'

'Of course they did. They were lovers, remember. I can't see my grandfather summoning a servant with a tray after indulging in something like our recent activities in this very bed.'

Colour rose in Flora's cheeks. 'No,' she agreed, trying to smooth the covers.

James leaned forward and caught her hand. 'Don't bother—waste of time.' He smiled wickedly in answer to the startled question in her eyes. 'Oh, yes, *mo cridhe*.' He stacked the tray and leaned over to put it on the floor. 'It's extraordinarily erotic to watch you eat, knowing exactly what made you hungry.'

Dawn arrived all too soon for Flora.

James slid out of bed and wrapped a towel round his hips. 'What will you do today?'

Flora lay back against the pillows, stretching luxuriously. 'I need just a couple of hours at the tower to finish the second water-colour, then I suppose I'd better clear up and move all my paraphernalia down from there.'

'I'll give you a hand.' He smiled, holding out an imperative hand. 'Come with me now! We can cook breakfast together at Ardlochan before I take you to the watchtower.'

'Won't Agnes think it strange to find me there so early?'

'She's not due for hours yet. Come on. You can sleep another day.'

Flora hesitated, then got out of bed. 'Why not? Only I'm having a bath first.'

Since James decided to join her the bath took rather longer than it should have done, and in the end he was obliged to drive at top speed to Ardlochan to make sure they had time for breakfast before Agnes put in an appearance.

Flora felt wildly happy as they drove through the sunlit morning, and sang as she cooked bacon and eggs in the Ardlochan kitchen while James went up to change. They ate at the kitchen table, talking non-stop, as though the night they'd shared had opened some new floodgate of rapport, and afterwards packed a basket with coffee and biscuits, and managed to leave for the tower before Agnes arrived to wonder what Miss Blair was doing at Ardlochan so early in the morning.

At the tower James saw Flora up to her eyrie, took her in his arms and kissed her at great length, promising to be back for her by noon.

'No hurry,' she assured him, touching a hand to his cheek. 'If I finish beforehand I might just stretch out and have a snooze.' She smiled, flushing. 'I didn't get any sleep last night, as you well know.'

He held her in a rib-cracking embrace for a moment, then detached himself reluctantly and swung himself down the ladder.

Flora waved to him from the window aperture, and stood watching the Land Rover out of sight with dreaming eyes. It was some time before she was in any state of mind to begin work. The finishing touches to the second water-colour took less than an hour to complete. Afterwards Flora tidied up while the paint dried, made herself as comfortable as possible on the rug James had provided, and poured herself some coffee. She leaned against the rough stone wall, immune to discomfort as she relived the night before. Her breath caught in her throat as she thought of James's lovemaking. Now, at last, she could understand

Genista Lyon's lifelong devotion to one man. If Charles Cameron had been a lover of James's calibre it was easily explained.

Just after eleven, long before she was expecting James, Flora heard a car approaching and leapt to the window eagerly, disappointed to see a smart, unfamiliar convertible approaching instead of the familiar Land Rover. But the driver was familiar enough. The smooth black head was unmistakable.

Flora scowled. What on earth was Catriona Urquhart doing here? She dodged away, hoping the visitor would think the place was deserted, but to her dismay Catriona disappeared inside the tower and began climbing the worn stone steps inside, puffing and panting as she negotiated the ladder on the final ascent to the top. Catriona scrambled ungracefully into the room at last, dusting down her white trousers as she nodded to Flora.

'Hello.'

'This *is* a surprise,' said Flora drily. 'Sorry I can't offer you a seat—unless you'd like to share my rug.'

Catriona shook her head. 'I'll only be a moment. I met James on his way to the sawmill. He said you were up here, so I thought I'd pop in for a chat.'

Thinking this was the most unlikely thing she'd ever heard, Flora gazed at her visitor sardonically and waited to learn the real reason for Catriona's visit.

The other woman picked her way gingerly over the splintered boards to peer at the drying water-colour. 'Hmm. Not bad, not bad. In the genes, I suppose. Old Miss Lyon was quite clever with a paintbrush too, so they say.'

'Oh, quite,' agreed Flora, wishing her visitor would take herself off. 'Lovely party last night. I enjoyed it very much. Thank you for inviting me.'

'Oh, don't thank me!' Catriona shrugged. 'It was Ewen's doing. Though I told him it was a lost cause. Poor fool! I told him he wouldn't stand a chance with James in the vicinity.'

'Your brother's very charming,' said Flora coldly. 'I like him very much.'

'I didn't climb up that terrifying ladder to talk about Ewen,' said Catriona, and swung round to face Flora, all pretence at civility abruptly abandoned. Her eyes glittered coldly, like green glass beads. 'I came on an errand of mercy, really.'

'Mercy?' Flora's eyebrows rose.

'Yes. It's high time you knew the truth.'

Flora leaned against the rough stone walls, hands in pockets. 'The truth about what, exactly?'

Catriona smiled scathingly. 'You really don't have a clue, do you?' She breathed in with deep satisfaction, savouring her next words as though they were honey on her tongue. 'You really believe James has fallen for you in a big way. I don't blame you. When he sets out to charm he can make a woman believe anything.'

Flora tensed. 'Do go on.'

'After waiting so long for old Miss Lyon to die James went totally berserk when he was told she'd willed the tenancy to you.' Catriona laughed mirthlessly. 'At first he was sure he could evict you legally, but Hamish Drummond said no. So Mrs Cameron advised James to use different tactics—to charm you into handing over the tenancy.'

Flora's stomach heaved, and she clenched her fists in her pockets, fighting to keep her face expressionless as she waited for Catriona to continue.

Catriona smiled spitefully. 'Surely you must have wondered why James is so keen to get it back, Miss Blair. For years he's been planning to turn Inch Cottage into a small hotel, a centre for fishing and walking and boating—all the usual tourist things, plus picturesque lodges in the woods for extra guests.' Catriona smoothed a hand over her hair. 'You were the only obstacle in the way, so James set out, in his own inimitable manner, to persuade you to hand the place back—any way he could.'

'And does he think he succeeded?' said Flora tonelessly.

Triumph gleamed in the green eyes. 'James was quite sure he had when I met him just now. He said that after last night it was an absolute certainty.' Her smile threatened Flora's hard-won composure badly. 'Did you really think you were any competition for *me*? Once my husband died it was always understood that James and I would marry. This little interlude with you was purely a means to an end, something to pass the time for James while I was in London. Those intimate little dinners of yours—how we laughed about them this morning. Surely you must have wondered why he never took you out anywhere? He had no intention of being seen in public with you. James, you see, likes to keep his image untarnished.' She smiled brilliantly. 'Oh, well, I probably won't see you again, so I'll say goodbye.'

'Goodbye, Mrs Urquhart,' said Flora steadily. 'Take care on your way down the ladder.'

'Oh, I shall,' Catriona assured her. '*Great* care, believe me.' And with a nonchalant little wave she swung herself over the top of the ladder and began the gruelling descent to the next floor.

Flora turned away to lean in the window aperture, staring blindly at the beauty below. Catriona Urquhart was lying, of course. She *had* to be lying. Yet her story was so horribly plausible. It all fitted together so well. Flora's teeth drew blood from her lower lip as thoughts of James's initial hostility flooded back, coupled with her own scepticism over his abrupt change of heart. But she *had* believed in it, for the simple reason that she'd wanted to so much.

Flora, fathoms-deep in agonising intro-spection, failed to hear the scraping noises at first. When they finally registered she spun round, just in time to see the ladder disappear from the opening, and in horror heard it crashing into the walls as it hurtled down inside the tower. With a screech she scrambled across the floor to peer down into the gloom, enraged at the sound of laughter floating up as Catriona made her way down the worn shallow steps to the ground.

Flora got back to the window aperture as fast as she could, yelling, '*Catriona*!' at the top of her voice as the other girl emerged into the sunshine.

But Catriona ran to her car, ignoring the shout from above, and with a roar of powerful engine disappeared into the distance at the wheel of her expensive car.

Flora slumped on the rug, fists clenched, shaking with rage. What did Catriona hope to gain by such a dirty, malevolent trick? Flora ground her teeth impotently, then forced herself to calm down as she gave herself a trenchant little lecture about waiting patiently until help arrived.

She wreathed her hands round her knees and laid her head down on them, her fury gradually replaced by sick reaction as she acknowledged the terrible credibility in Catriona's story. Steeling herself, Flora went over every detail of the short time she'd known James, from the moment of their first hostile encounter right up to the impassioned events of the previous night. For her their lovemaking had been the most magical experience of her life. But for James it could just have been a typically male way of gaining his own ends. In which case it was a wonder he'd managed to keep quiet on the subject of Inch Cottage as he'd made love to her. When, thought Flora bitterly, had he intended to ask for it outright? Today, when he came for her? Or possibly he'd had another night of passion in mind, as a sort of bonus, to make doubly sure she was willing to give him anything he asked, the tenancy included.

Flora jumped to her feet in revulsion, desperate now to escape. She peered down from the doorway to the floor below, but one look was enough. Without a ladder, or at the very least a rope, there was no possible hope of getting down from the tower unaided.

On the way back to her rug she tripped over her sketchbook, and paused, eyeing it. She was in no mood for water-colour. But she had charcoal and paper, and endless time to kill. She lifted down the almost dry water-colour and set her sketchbook on the easel instead. With swift, slashing strokes she began to draw, pouring out her anger and grief on page after page, so immersed in her task that she forgot the time until her dry throat reminded her of the coffee. As she poured a little into a beaker she glanced at her watch, and frowned, startled.

James had promised to come at noon, but it was now almost two o'clock. Her emotions had see-sawed while she was drawing. One moment she longed for escape without seeing James, the next she was itching to confront him, to demand whether Catriona had told the truth. But of course she had. The things she'd said were only

too easy to verify. Flora's mouth tightened.
James was certain to lie about his motives in
making love to her, of course. On the other
hand he just might be honest enough to admit
that his sole intention all along had been to
charm her into handing Inch Cottage back to
him.

Abruptly Flora lost her zest for sketching, her
emotion burned out, channelled on to the
paper. She went to the window and stared long-
ingly at the road to Ardlochan, but there was
no sign of James. Where in heaven's name *was*
he? She was seized by an overpowering urge to
escape, the stone walls of the tower suddenly
closing in on her like a prison. Swallowing hard,
Flora let herself down on the rug and leaned
her head wearily against the wall, feeling the
effect of her sleepless night and Catriona's revelations. Whether Catriona was lying or not,
the poisoned seeds of doubt she'd sown flourished more vigorously in Flora's mind the longer
she dwelt on them. Last night she'd forgotten
everything but the joy of being in James's arms,
but today she felt cheap, used. She curled up
on the rug, too miserable to care about comfort
as she pillowed her head on her arm, and at last
fell into a troubled, uneasy doze. When she
woke with a start the light was very different.
In horror she saw it was after six. She struggled

to her feet and stared from the tower window in anguish. But the road girdling the loch remained deserted as it wound away in the direction of Ardlochan.

CHAPTER NINE

WHILE the light lasted Flora was able, just barely, to cope with the loneliness and claustrophobia closing in on her. But as the evening dragged on and the light began to fail she felt the first onset of panic. James must have had an accident. It was the only possible explanation. He would never leave her here like this, that much she was certain, whatever his motives in laying siege to her. At the word siege she gave a hysterical little laugh, which bounced back with such a ghostly echo from the walls that she clapped a hand over her mouth, trembling.

She was certainly besieged now, cut off from the ground by a drop of so many feet that she had no hope of getting down without help. And help, it seemed, wasn't forthcoming.

Flora began reciting poetry, everything she'd ever learned or read that she could remember. But eventually her voice cracked and the tears came, at which point she gave in to despair. A long time later she fell asleep again through sheer exhaustion, and dreamed vivid, frightening dreams, and woke with a gasp to the bitter fantasy of hearing James call her name.

Then the sound came again—'*Flora!*'—and she gave a choked sob and struggled to her feet, staggering a little as she made for the oblong of starlight outlined by the window aperture.

'James, *James!*' she screeched, and leaned out perilously far, overcome with relief as she saw the headlights of a stationary vehicle. She heard James call her name again, the hollowness of the sound telling her he was already inside the tower. She crawled across the floor in the dark and leaned through the opening, her spirits rising as a faint glimmer of light indicated that James was making his way up the steps of the first two floors with a torch. She heard him curse, and called hoarsely to him.

'The ladder's gone.'

'So I see,' he yelled. 'Is that Catriona's doing?'

'Yes.'

James spat out something unintelligible, then shone the torch up in Flora's face. 'Are you all right?'

'More or less,' she croaked.

'Hang on. I'll go back down for the ladder. Stay still. Don't move.'

Flora could have cried as she saw the glimmer of light disappear. She hugged her arms across her chest, her teeth chattering with cold and fatigue, finding it hard to endure even the small wait while James hauled the ladder up for her to get down.

He was a long time. It seemed hours before she saw the light returning and then James's voice, hoarse with rage.

'The bloody ladder's just a pile of firewood! It must have disintegrated as it hit the walls on the way down. Flora, can you hang on a little while longer?'

Flora, speechless with disappointment, took a while to answer him. 'I'll have to, won't I?' she called at last. 'How much longer?'

'Only as long as it takes to drive back to the house for a ladder,' he shouted. 'I wish I could leave you the torch, but if I tried to throw it up it might break.'

'Then keep it,' she cried. 'Only hurry, please. I'm freezing.'

'I'm gone,' he yelled, and started back down the stairs at breakneck speed.

After the Land Rover had hurtled off down the track everything was deadly quiet, the darkness more threatening now than before. Afraid to crawl back across the floor for the rug, Flora huddled against the cold stone wall and concentrated doggedly on the fact that in a short time she'd be out of this place and in a warm bed, and as soon as humanly possible after that she'd be on her way to France.

But to her dismay, now that help was so close at hand, she was horribly conscious of the noises of the night. She could hear slight rustlings and scrapings from below, and a breeze that soughed through the window aperture with a sound so like moaning that she stiffened, her heart thumping as she suddenly remembered the story of the fated Lady Mariotta. Flora closed her eyes tightly, furious that her mind had decided to dredge up such a choice titbit to plague her now her ordeal was so nearly over. She told herself again and again that the sounds were field-mice and other wildlife, and the wind was just a wind, and not the despairing moans of a woman long since dead. Nevertheless her eyes remained tight shut until the welcome sound of James's Land Rover shattered the night.

Flora hauled herself stiffly to her feet, aching in every bone as she leaned out to see lights and voices. James had brought help, and suddenly things got hectic. Once he'd hauled himself up to her level he took only a second or two to assure himself Flora was in one piece, then began giving terse orders she found quite impossible to obey. Her feet and legs were so stiff and cold that they refused to function, whereupon James threw her over his shoulder and climbed down, deaf to her terrified protests, while willing hands from below held the ladder steady, then received her in a respectful embrace until he could carry her down the worn, perilous steps to safety.

For a while everything was blurred. Flora was vaguely aware of James talking to another man, of being wrapped in a wonderfully warm rug and fastened into her seat in the Land Rover before she relapsed into a grey, twilight world of semi-consciousness, only emerging from it when the vehicle stopped.

'Where are we?' she demanded feebly.

'Ardlochan,' said James, undoing her seatbelt. 'You'll stay here the night.'

'I will not!' She pushed at his hands. 'Take me to Inch Cottage, please.'

'Flora, don't be silly,' he said impatiently, but she shied away as he tried to pull her from her seat.

'Inch Cottage,' she said through her teeth, and the man in the back slid to the ground, wished Miss Blair a very good night, and hoped she would take no harm from her experience.

Flora, unable to see her rescuer's face in the darkness, thanked him politely, and by sheer good luck managed to slot her seatbelt back into its socket.

'Flora,' said James grimly. 'This is nonsense. My mother's waiting with hot soup and the electric blanket blazing on one of the spare beds. Be sensible——'

'How kind,' said Flora frigidly. 'But I shan't trouble her. I want to go back to the cottage—if you'd be good enough to drive me there.'

James had a muttered exchange with the other man, then stalked round the Land Rover and got in the driving seat in grim silence. No further word was spoken until he drew up at Inch Cottage, by which time Flora was light-headed with fatigue and tension.

James leapt from his seat and strode round to help her out.

'I can walk,' she said with dignity.

'I'll take your arm just the same,' he retorted. 'Where's your key?'

Flora fumbled through the folds of the rug to the back pocket of her jeans and handed him the key, then stood, muffled like an Indian squaw, while James opened the door and switched on the lights.

'I'll be fine now,' she said unsteadily, then blenched as James took her by the shoulders and turned her towards the hall mirror. The overhead light was merciless, showing up a filthy, pallid face with black rings under the eyes and hair escaping in witch-locks from the braid. Flora shuddered.

'Quite so,' said James. 'Give me that rug and let me carry you upstairs. We need to talk, urgently, but first I want you safely in bed with a hot drink and something to eat.'

'No!' said Flora, pulling away.

James, whose appearance was little better than hers after scrambling about in the tower, glared at her, frustrated. 'What do you mean, no? Give me that rug.'

Flora clutched it around her obstinately. 'You can make me some tea, if you like, but I'll get myself upstairs under my own steam.'

James breathed in, his nostrils flaring. 'As you like.' He stood, arms folded, watching her as she stumbled upstairs.

Flora went through the bedroom and straight into the bathroom, locking the door behind her. She discarded the rug, turned on the bath-taps, then stripped off her clothes in distaste, threw them into the linen basket and climbed into the steaming, scented water with a sigh of relief. She lay back, eyes closed, rubbing shampoo in her loosened hair before she let it float in the water, resentful when only a few moments later James hammered on the door.

'Time you came out of there,' he ordered.

Wearily Flora hauled herself out of the bath and towelled herself dry, then reached for the dressing-gown hanging on the door.

'James?' she called through the door. 'Are you there?'

'Of course I'm here,' he said impatiently. What the hell are you doing? Hurry up.'

'I'm cold. Pass my nightgown in, please.'

'Where is it?'

'Under my pillow.' Flora waited, shivering, then James tapped on the door.

'It's not here, Flora. I forgot to tell you. All your clothes are missing. I was told you were, too. I had a message to say you'd left in a hurry because of some crisis at home.'

Flora frowned, mystified. 'I don't understand.'

'I'll explain, but not through a locked door,' he said forcibly. 'Wrap yourself in a towel and come out.'

Apathetically she shrugged into the dressing-gown, belted it tightly then opened the door to James, who looked grim and forbidding as his eyes searched her face.

'I suppose Catriona told you I'd gone?' Flora enquired coldly, and got into bed, feeling better once she was propped against pillows with the covers up to her chin. 'Surely you thought it was rather a coincidence that she turned up at

the watchtower today just as I received some
mysterious message from home?'

'I didn't know she'd been anywhere near the
tower.' James poured soup from an insulated
flask into a beaker and handed it to her. 'Only
the canned variety, but drink it while it's hot.
You look like a ghost.'

Flora grimaced. 'Don't mention ghosts.' With
a sigh she manoeuvred herself upright to drink
the soup. 'If Catriona didn't tell you I'd gone,
who did?'

'Agnes.' James sat on the edge of the *chaise-
longue*, leaning forward slightly, his hands
clasped between his knees. 'I was late getting
away from the sawmill, but so filthy I needed
a shower before I went to collect you. When I
reached home Agnes said there was a message
from the housekeeper at Strathroy. Apparently
Ewen Urquhart had met Archie Lennox the
postman on his way to Inch Cottage with an
urgent message for Miss Blair, about illness in
the family. According to the housekeeper Ewen
delivered the message to you at the watchtower,
drove you back to Inch Cottage for your clothes
and gave you a lift to Glasgow to catch a train.'

Flora's heavy eyes narrowed over the rim of
the mug. 'That's pure fabrication!'

James nodded grimly. 'Obviously.' He looked
at her levelly. 'After what happened between us

last night I was certain you'd have left some kind of message for me, so I drove straight here to look for it.'

James made it plain he'd been thunder-struck to find no word from Flora. He'd checked that all her belongings were gone then driven back to Ardlochan and rung the Urquharts to see if they could shed light on the mystery. The housekeeper had answered, informing James that Catriona had driven her parents to visit friends for a couple of days while the house was put back in order after the party, and Mr Ewen had taken a Miss Blair to Glasgow.

'It all seemed to fit,' he concluded, and got up to pour tea from the tray beside the bed. 'As there was no message, I took it you'd had time to think, regretted what happened between us, and broke it to me by taking off without leaving an address.'

Flora exchanged her soup-mug for the teacup he gave her. 'And all the time I was a prisoner in the tower, and Catriona on her way to some unknown destination, gloating over my predicament every inch of the way. Charming lady.' She eyed James questioningly. 'How did you find out where I was?'

When Ewen Urquhart had returned to Strathroy in the small hours he had found a message to say that Mr Cameron had rung, very anxious about a Miss Blair. Ewen, no less anxious himself, had rung James at two in the morning, demanding to know what was wrong.

'You can imagine my reaction when I discovered he knew nothing about you *or* any crisis! When he heard you were missing he went up like a rocket and was all for jumping in his car to look for you himself.' James moved to sit on the edge of the bed. 'I soon put a stop to that. Angus will give him a ring to say you were safe.'

'Angus?'

'He came to your rescue with me tonight. He's one of the gillies on the estate.'

'Please thank him for me.'

'You can do that yourself.'

'I won't have time.' Flora gave him a long, unsmiling look. 'Once I track down my clothes I'm leaving.'

'*Why*?' James's voice hardened. 'I appreciate what you must have felt, shut up in the tower, but something else is wrong, Flora. What is it?'

Without emotion Flora put him in the picture about Catriona's visit and her removal of the ladder. 'But before she went she told me a very interesting story.'

He stiffened. 'Story?'

'One with an unhappy ending. The real story of why James Cameron laid siege to Flora Blair.'

He got up, standing with arms folded as he loomed over her. 'I suppose she told you I made a play for you to get Inch Cottage back.'

Flora nodded. 'Catriona said you plan to turn it into some kind of holiday centre. Is that true?'

He nodded reluctantly. 'In essence, yes, but——'

'Then there's no more to be said.' Flora's mouth twisted in distaste. 'It explains why you tried to rush me into bed that first night. You were on fire to possess the house, not me!'

'No!' he said fiercely. 'You're wrong. It's true I wanted Inch Cottage, but not as much as I've wanted *you* from the moment I first set eyes on you.'

She held her voice steady with effort. 'I suppose that should be a comfort, but it doesn't alter the fact that you deliberately set out to—to make me fall in love with you. Once I was putty in your hands you were confident I'd hand back Inch Cottage on a plate.' Suddenly reaction to the entire day washed over her in a wave. James started towards her as he saw tears, but she fended him off violently. 'Don't touch me!'

He halted, his fists clenched. 'Don't look at me like that! Let me explain, Flora.'

'What is there to explain?' She rubbed at her eyes mercilessly. 'Though what really hurts is that your mother was in on it too. I—I liked her so much——'

'My mother is blameless,' he interrupted, his eyes blazing. 'Catriona distorted the truth. Not very much—just enough to paint my mother and myself black in your eyes without ever actually lying. Mother did say I was a fool to antagonise you. She was sure you were a reasonable young woman, and if I told you exactly why I needed Inch Cottage you were more than likely to relinquish any claim to it. She told me from the first I was wrong to keep you in the dark about my plans.' Sudden colour stained his cheekbones. 'But my pleasure in the siege was so intense I wouldn't listen. I was afraid that if you did hand the tenancy back you'd leave before——'

'Before you made it to my bed,' said Flora, in words that hung in the silence like icicles.

The colour drained from James's face, leaving it drawn and bleak. 'Today I meant to tell you everything, including my plans for Inch Cottage—how its development will provide employment for young people forced to leave the area to find work.'

'Why didn't you say so at the start?' said Flora passionately. 'Why did you have to go through all that rigmarole to soften me up?'

He met her accusing eyes without flinching. 'Every day I meant to tell you the truth, and every day I put it off another day for the sheer pleasure of keeping you here. It was another of my famed mistakes. Now you're looking at me as though you hate me.'

'Is it any wonder?' Her eyes flashed coldly. 'I lay there in that horrible tower today feeling I'd been used. I felt betrayed—dirty.'

'Only because of the way you'd found out!'

'Was Catriona's version so very far from the actual truth, then?' she threw at him. 'No matter how you wrap it up, James Cameron, you made an utter fool of me. I'm not denying the attraction between us, but you used it for your own ends, and I despise you for it. Now please go away and leave me alone!'

He started for her purposefully, but she flung up a hand.

'No! You've had your say. All I ask now is that you track down my belongings so that I can get away from here. As far as I'm concerned you can have your precious Inch Cottage, gift-wrapped. I never want to set foot in the place again!' Flora turned her face into the pillow and yanked the covers over her ears.

She felt James touch her shoulder and flinched away, and after a tense pause she heard the door close as he left the room. Flora sat up in bed, tears streaming down her face as she heard the outer door bang and the Land Rover start up outside. James, as requested, had left her alone with her misery for what remained of the night.

Flora woke next morning feeling like death. Instant recall of the night before did nothing to brighten a day that was grey and overcast to match her mood. The sunshine days of her idyll were over in more ways than one. Yet until her clothes were found, she thought in despair, she had no way of leaving. A knock on the bedroom door brought her bolt upright in bed, clutching the covers to her chin.

'Who is it?' she said coldly.

'It's only me, Miss Blair,' said a familiar voice, and to Flora's astonishment Jean MacPhail popped her head round the door.

'Jean!' Flora could have hugged the friendly, smiling woman. 'Oh, how lovely to see you again. I didn't know you were back.'

'We came last night, but you weren't here, of course,' said Jean, depositing a laden tray on the bedside table. 'Now let me push those pillows behind you and make you comfortable, deary, so you can eat this nice breakfast I've brought.'

'Oh, Jean,' said Flora shakily. 'This is so kind of you—but I'm not ill.'

'Then it's a miracle you're not, lassie! When Mr James told me what happened I could hardly believe my ears. I never heard of such a thing, shut up alone in that old ruin until the small hours.' Jean settled the tray across Flora's lap, shaking her head in disapproval. 'Now eat up. You'll soon feel better.'

Flora doubted that porridge and poached eggs were a cure for what ailed her, but under Jean's relentless eye she ate a little of the food and drank strong, reviving tea while Jean regaled her with tales of the bonny new grandson.

'I've brought your luggage up again,' said Jean casually, astonishing Flora. 'You won't be well enough to travel today, so I brought your cases in the house. Donald found them in the boot of the car when he was cleaning it this morning.'

Clever little Catriona, thought Flora balefully.

'Now you get up and have a nice bath,' said Jean, taking the tray. 'Then come back to bed. Mrs Cameron will be here soon to see how you are.'

'No! I can't see anyone. I really must leave today——' began Flora, but Jean interrupted her briskly.

'Have you seen yourself in the glass? You're not fit to leave your bed, let alone travel. But with me to see to things you'll be fine in a day or two. I'll bring the cases up and find a nightie for you.'

Flora waited until Jean was gone then slid hastily out of bed and into the bathroom, her head pounding dully as she took a quick bath and tidied herself up. One look in the mirror made it plain why Jean had vetoed any plans for travelling. She surveyed her red-lidded eyes and ashen pallor with distaste, then put on the cotton nightshirt Jean passed discreetly round the door and allowed herself to be shepherded back to bed.

Jean smoothed the covers, clucking her tongue as she eyed Flora's face. 'Och, you're that pale, deary. Mrs Cameron's here but I'll tell her she mustn't stay long. Do you feel bad? Perhaps I should call the doctor.'

Flora shook her head in alarm. 'No! I just need a bit of time to get over my fright last night, Jean, that's all.' She smiled brightly. 'I was even hearing ghostly noises by the time I was rescued.'

Jean nodded matter-of-factly. 'That would be Lady Mariotta.'

'I was only joking!'

Jean looked unconvinced. 'Aye, well . . . I'll tell Mrs Cameron to come up.'

Flora lay tense in the great bed, uneasy at the prospect of seeing James's mother, but the moment Isobel Cameron walked in the room the concern in her eyes put paid to Flora's qualms.

'My dear child, how do you feel?' exclaimed Mrs Cameron, and sat down in the chair Jean had placed ready beside the bed.

'Just tired, really,' Flora assured her, trying to smile.

'As well you might be!' Mrs Cameron looked very grave. 'I was appalled when James told me what happened. Catriona Urquhart deserves a good spanking. She's been utterly ruined, of course, first by her parents and then her husband, and behaves like a spoiled, spiteful child when something she wants is denied her. Which is no excuse for putting you in danger in such a criminally irresponsible way. Heaven knows how long you might have been there if Ewen hadn't contacted James.'

'James genuinely thought I'd left, then,' said Flora.

Mrs Cameron nodded. 'He was devastated. Particularly when he thought you'd left no word for him. He rushed over here to Inch Cottage to search for a note, then returned home in such a state I hardly dared say a word for fear of getting my head bitten off.' She waited expectantly, then sighed when Flora made no response. 'Perhaps this is the time to say I've come here as an envoy, on a peace mission of sorts.'

'Please,' said Flora, stirring restively. 'I'd rather——'

'Hear me out, my dear,' said Mrs Cameron gently. 'First of all, I did *not* make friends with you to coax you out of Inch Cottage. I asked you to dinner at James's request, certainly, but my invitation to tea was a genuine desire to get to know you better once I'd met you.'

Flora gazed at her uncertainly, badly wanting to believe her. Mrs Cameron, sensing it, went on to explain that she'd advised James from the first to be honest about Inch Cottage, to explain why he needed it and to propose some suitable kind of compromise on the tenancy, even to the point of a financial arrangement if necessary.

'Having met you, I was sure you'd be sympathetic once you knew what he intended.' Mrs Cameron smiled wryly. 'But James was madly in love for the first time in his life, and men in such a state are strangers to common sense.'

Flora's stomach muscles contracted violently at the thought of James in love. She looked away, colouring. 'He told you he was?'

'No need. I'm not too old to recognise the signs!' Mrs Cameron sighed again. 'Unfortunately Catriona recognised them too. After seeing you with James at the dance she drove over early yesterday and told James she'd always intended him to marry *her* once she was a rich widow, and suggested offering you a lump sum for Inch Cottage to "get rid of you", as she put it.'

Flora's eyes widened. 'What did he say to that?'

'He refused with such force that Catriona flew into a rage and promised him he'd be sorry.' Mrs Cameron looked grim for a moment. 'Which he was, very quickly, when he thought you'd gone for good without a word.'

'But what did she hope to gain by playing such a trick on me?'

'I don't suppose she even thought it out. Revenge, possibly—or retaliation for James's rejection. Whatever her motive it was a criminally dangerous thing to do. You could easily have fallen and broken a leg—or worse.' She shuddered. 'It doesn't bear thinking about.'

Belatedly her attention turned to the room, her dark eyes gleaming as they travelled slowly over the flamboyant decoration.

'Good gracious, Flora. I was so worried by your pale face when I arrived I didn't notice the room. I've never set foot in it before.' She chuckled, and waved a hand at the portrait of her father-in-law. 'He really created a love-nest for his darling, didn't he? And right on his own doorstep, too.'

Flora smiled, feeling slightly better. 'A law unto himself.'

'Very much so. The laird of Ardlochan could do no wrong in these parts.' She paused, her smile fading. 'Which brings me to his grandson. James has recovered your equipment from the tower. I am instructed to ask whether he may return it to you himself later on.'

Flora shook her head violently. 'I'd rather he didn't.'

The dark eyes shadowed. 'I haven't been successful in pleading his cause, then?'

'It isn't that, Mrs Cameron.'

'If it's not, am I allowed to ask why you won't see him?'

Flora thought carefully before answering. 'The time I've spent here has been a pleasant interlude in my life. But now it's over and time

I went back where I belong. I never intended staying more than a few days.'

'Which is no reason to go off without seeing James,' said Mrs Cameron gently. 'If it was just an interlude, at least round it off properly.'

In the end Flora gave in, feeling much better by the time her visitor departed. She had hated the thought of Isobel Cameron's complicity in the campaign to get her out of Inch Cottage. But the fact remained that James, however much he tried to deny it, had deliberately embarked on a campaign of his own. His besieging of the citadel had been a pleasure to them both, thought Flora bleakly, but never the least necessary. Victory had been his all along.

Much against Jean's wishes Flora got up once Mrs Cameron had gone, but after an afternoon spent sitting listlessly in the garden had so little appetite for the meal Jean prepared that she allowed herself to be bullied back to bed.

'I'll let Mr James in,' said Jean firmly. 'I'll give Donald his supper while your visitor is here then come back and spend the night.'

Flora agreed meekly, then lay tense against the pillows, waiting for James.

He arrived punctually as usual. Flora heard Jean let him in, and the small commotion of transferring her painting equipment from the car into the house before Jean popped her head round the bedroom door.

'Mr James is here. Shall I tell him to come up?'

Flora nodded dumbly and sat bolt upright against the pillows, her nerves raw and quivering by the time James arrived in the bedroom.

'Hello, Flora,' he said quietly, as he came in. 'How do you feel?'

'A bit tired.' She waved him to the chair his mother had occupied earlier.

James sat down, his stern male presence alien in the frivolous room as he looked long and hard at Flora. 'You're deathly pale.'

'Yes. Odd, isn't it? My tan seems to have disappeared.'

'You've spent too much time in the tower lately——' He stopped, his jaw tightening, and she smiled coldly.

'How very true.'

They looked at each other in taut silence.

'It's plain my mother's mission was unsuccessful,' he said grimly at last. 'You still feel hostile towards us.'

'Not to your mother.'

'But I've been tried and found guilty,' he said with bitterness.

Flora shrugged indifferently. 'Surely that doesn't matter to you? Your siege was successful. The citadel is yours.'

His eyes lit with a sudden heat and she smiled scornfully. 'I'm referring to Inch Cottage.'

His mouth tightened. 'Then you're convinced my motive for making love to you was mercenary.'

She thought about it, then shook her head. 'Not entirely. I think what happened between us was a pleasurable experience for you, whatever the reasons behind it.'

'The only reason behind it, dammit, was the fact that I wanted to make love to you more than anything I'd ever wanted in my entire life,' he said violently, then took himself in hand with effort. 'My mother says you intend leaving tomorrow. Is that true?'

'Yes.'

'You're going home?'

'No, to France,' said Flora sweetly. 'I'm joining—a group a friends in the Perigord,' she added, not quite brave enough to mention Tom Harvey.

His eyes burned in his taut face. 'Is this a sudden decision?'

'Of course not. I planned it months ago.' She shrugged. 'I came here first solely because my aunt asked me to. I never meant to stay so long.'

'I see,' he said grimly. 'So everything tha[t]
happened between us was just a sort of sexua[l]
Highland fling as far as you're concerned.'

She winced, her lids dropping to hide he[r]
eyes. 'No. You know it wasn't. But I just can'[t]
forgive you for not being honest with me. Al[l]
you ever had to do was tell me about the hote[l]
and why you needed the cottage and...' Sh[e]
halted, unable to go on.

'And what?' said James swiftly. 'Would yo[u]
have stayed?'

'Probably not.' She raised her eyes to mee[t]
his. 'I'm not Genista Lyon, and you're no[t]
Charles Cameron. Your place is here. Min[e]
isn't.' She shrugged. 'Anyway, Inch Cottage i[s]
now officially yours. This afternoon I wrote t[o]
Hamish Drummond confirming the fact tha[t]
I've relinquished all claim to it. Your effort[s]
were superfluous as it happens, James. I alway[s]
intended to hand the tenancy back once m[y]
holiday was over.'

He stared at her malevolently. 'Then why al[l]
that charade about the sprig of broom and th[e]
feu duty?'

Flora coloured slightly. 'You're not the onl[y]
one with a temper. I lost mine that mornin[g]
you came gunning for me. If you'd bee[n]
friendly and reasonable I would never hav[e]
thought of it. But you were so overbearing an[d]

obnoxious I thought it would be fun to make you fry a little until I left for France.'

James rose to his feet, his face like a mask. 'So neither of us is totally blameless. If you'd told me from the start what you had in mind it would have saved a lot of trouble.'

'True,' she agreed. 'Your siege was never really necessary.'

The look in his eyes dried her mouth. 'Ah, but it was aimed at your heart, Flora, not Inch Cottage. Which only shows what a bloody fool I've been. I laid siege to something which doesn't exist.' He strode to the door, then turned to look at her. 'Goodbye, Flora. Or perhaps I should say *bon voyage*.' And with a formal nod he closed the door behind him and left her alone with only the echoes of a long-dead romance for company.

CHAPTER TEN

FLORA never reached France. A combination of will-power and determination got her to the train at Fort William, but after the worried MacPhails had seen her settled and waved her off on her journey Flora knew she'd do well to get as far as Gloucestershire, let alone the Perigord. Afterwards she remembered alarmingly little of changing trains at Glasgow, other than a phone call to her father, asking him to meet her at the station in Cheltenham. When she stumbled from the train at last Edward Blair relieved his ashen daughter of her luggage, hugged her close then drove her home as fast as possible to deliver her into her mother's care.

Lucy Blair's opinion of Scottish holidays which led to raging influenza was repeated almost daily once her daughter was on the road to recovery. Flora, thinking it unwise to mention that heartache was retarding the process, obediently took vitamins, ate unenthusiastically of nourishing meals, made apologetic phone calls to a very irate Tom Harvey and did her best to get fit enough to return to school. But she remained obstinately reticent about her stay in Scotland. Her parents were naturally curious about the place which had drawn Genista Lyon back to it year after year, and even more about the man who been her lover. Flora gave them a brief account of Charles Cameron, and described the beauty of Ardlochan, said the Camerons had been kind and hospitable and diverted her father's interest by talking about the proposed conversion of Inch Cottage into a small, select holiday complex.

Flora's convalescence was slow, and suffered a severe set-back when Tom Harvey came to visit her, full of recriminations about his ruined holiday. Flora heard him out, gazing at his irate, freckled face and shock of fair hair, utterly depressed because the face she yearned for was dark and forceful and last seen with an expression of furious distaste on it. She apologised to Tom, sent him on his way with a firm refusal to let him come again, then gave in when her mother put her back to bed for a day or two before allowing her up to resume her convalescence.

Eventually Flora felt sufficiently restored to make an appointment with the London gallery which had handled her aunt's work. Marcus

Beauchamp, son of the owner of Beauchamp Galleries, was an attractive man with smooth brown hair and gold-rimmed glasses. He expressed his sympathy on the death of Miss Lyon, then turned to Flora's work with flattering interest.

Flora showed him the two water-colours she'd painted at the watchtower, holding her breath as Marcus placed them on adjacent easels. He looked from one to the other at length.

'I like them very much, Miss Blair,' he said at last. 'But I wonder if water-colour is your normal medium?'

'It's not.' She opened her portfolio. 'These sketches are more my style. I did a series of them with an old watchtower as the focal-point.'

Marcus Beauchamp warmed considerably as he examined the bold, starkly simple studies. 'These are good. Highly individual. I like them.'

'More than the other two?'

The water-colours, he informed her, were very attractive, and would probably sell for a respectable sum. But the charcoal studies were something out of the ordinary.

'Amazing how you've managed to invest such drama into them, even a certain hint of the macabre.' He smiled at her. 'Is the place haunted?'

'Oh, yes. At least one accredited spectre.' If not two, she thought glumly. After her incarceration something of herself probably haunted the place to keep Lady Mariotta company. 'Well, Mr Beauchamp? Are you interested?'

'I could be.' He smiled in a way which told her his interest was by no means limited to her work. 'Let's discuss it over lunch.'

Flora enjoyed eating in an expensive restaurant with an escort who was not only attractive but an expert in the field which interested her most. Marcus talked at length about Genista Lyon, surprising Flora with the news that the artist's work had escalated in value quite considerably since her death. And to round off the meal Marcus Beauchamp confirmed that the gallery would display Flora's work to see how it caught the public's fancy.

'Not the water-colours,' she said abruptly. 'I'm keeping those.'

'Sentimental attachment?'

'Something like that.' She finished her coffee in thoughtful silence, then looked up. 'Mr Beauchamp——'

'Marcus, please.'

She smiled. 'What would you say, Marcus, if I told you I'd recently seen a set of a dozen Genista Lyon water-colours entirely new to you?'

The keen blue eyes narrowed to an acquis-
itive gleam behind their lenses. 'I'd say give me
the owner's telephone number!'

Flora was glad to get back to teaching, and from
the first day of the autumn term threw herself
into every possible activity, over and above her
normal teaching schedule. For the first time
since her headlong flight from Ardlochan she
began to sleep better, to pass hours at a time
without thinking of James. Gradually she began
to feel she might even get over him one day,
and congratulated herself on the recuperative
powers of her besieged heart.

On a Friday a few weeks into the term the
headmistress's secretary interrupted the last
period of the day, a lecture on the Pre-
Raphaelites to the Lower Sixth, to say Miss
Blair was wanted in Dr Chalmers's study.

Flora gave her pupils a chapter to read on
Millais, then made for the head's study, mystified. Dr Chalmers was an erudite, magnetic
lady whom Flora admired enormously, but not
given to cosy chats in her study during school
hours. Flora paused in the hall, swallowing. Her
parents! Something must be wrong. She raced
up the stairs, her heart pounding.

She knocked on the heavy oak door and went
in, looking anxiously at the dark, striking

woman seated behind a beautiful Georgian desk. 'You wanted me, Dr Chalmers?' Then Flora's stomach gave a great, sickening lurch as she saw the tall man standing motionless between the windows.

The headmistress rose to her feet briskly. 'Come in, Flora. You have a visitor. Since Mr Cameron arrived only a few minutes ago I suggested he wait for you here. I'll leave you to talk in private and get someone to dismiss your class.'

'Thank you,' said Flora mechanically, her heart banging madly against her ribs as she looked at James. When the door closed behind Dr Chalmers he moved towards Flora, holding out his hand, a closed, wary expression on his face.

'Hello, Flora. Are you better?'

She looked at the hand but couldn't trust herself to touch it. 'Yes. Thank you. How did you know I was ill?'

James let his hand fall, his face darkening. 'I've been to see your parents. They told me you went straight home from Ardlochan instead of making for France.'

James had been to see her *parents*? 'Yes,' said Flora. 'I had flu.'

'You were quite ill, according to your mother.'

'She was rather cross about it.' Flora gave him a social little smile. 'In her view holidays should improve one's health, not the reverse.'

His mouth twisted. 'Did you tell her about your incarceration in the watchtower?'

'No.' She looked away. 'It would have led to explanations I had no intention of making.'

There was silence in the room, broken at last by a bell which signalled a frenetic burst of activity in the building as lessons finished for the day.

'This is impossible. Are you free this evening?' James looked at her urgently. 'I must talk to you.'

Flora kept her eyes on the playing fields visible from the window. 'I'm on duty at prep.'

'After that, then,' he said impatiently. 'I'll take you to a late supper somewhere.'

Flora turned speculative eyes on him. Although James was wearing the dark suit of the dinner party, he exuded a powerful, outdoor air of masculinity very much at odds with the cloistered, all-female atmosphere of the school building.

'I suppose I could,' she said grudgingly, 'if only out of curiosity. What brings you to this part of the world, James?'

'I could tell you more easily over a meal than in here.' He smiled wryly. 'Your Dr Chalmers is a formidable lady. I got the impression I wasn't expected to stay long.'

'Then you'd better go.'

'I will—as soon as you've promised to dine with me tonight.' His eyes locked with hers, telling her he had no intention of leaving until the promise was given.

Flora shrugged. 'Since you've come so far out of your way to see me I suppose I can't refuse. I won't be free until eight. But don't come for me,' she added hastily. 'I'll drive down to the lodge at the main gates and wait for you there.'

'Whatever you say.' James raised an eyebrow. 'Will you see me out? Or do I run the gauntlet alone as I make my escape?'

'I'm afraid you do.' Flora had no intention of letting any of her pupils see her with James. 'I'll stay here until you're well away.'

Inevitably she was forced to put up with a lot of teasing in the staffroom once Jane, the head's secretary, gave everyone a graphic description of the visitor. Flora passed it off by saying that James Cameron needed to see her on business.

'Something to do with the official hand-over of the cottage my great-aunt left me. It's on his estate,' she said with perfect truth, and went off to supervise a session of prep before getting ready for her evening with James.

It was late before Flora managed a hasty shower and slid into the dress worn to the dinner party at Ardlochan House. She tied her hair at the nape of her neck with a scarf, added the amber earrings, then snatched up her bag, raced down the back stairs and reached the car park without meeting anyone, to her relief.

She drove down the winding mile of drive, her heart giving an involuntary thump when she spotted the Aston Martin waiting near the lodge. She parked her Mini and hurried towards James, who was standing with the passenger door open, dressed in cords and a suede jacket over a roll-neck sweater.

'Sorry,' she panted. 'I'm late. Prep went on a bit tonight.'

'You came in the end so I'm not complaining.'

Flora looked at him curiously as he got in the car. 'Did you think I might not?'

'The thought did occur to me now and then while I was waiting.' He smiled bleakly. ' After the way we parted I wouldn't have blamed you for not bothering to turn up, Flora.'

'But I said I'd come.'

'You might have thought better of it.' James glanced at her as he started the car. 'I could have taken you to my hotel for dinner, but I hoped you'd settle for something less formal. I've been told there's a very good pub called the Green Man not far from here. A bit off the beaten track, so hopefully you shouldn't run into anyone you know.'

'It wouldn't matter if I did.'

'Possibly not. But I want a private talk with you, without distraction, Flora.' He gave her a very bright, sidelong glance, then returned his attention to the road.

The Green Man was a popular place, and the bar very crowded, but by the time their late supper was over Flora was virtually alone with James in the deserted dining-room.

'I thought I'd wait until we were free from interruption before dispensing with the small talk,' he remarked, watching Flora refill their coffee-cups. He glanced round him, but the few remaining diners were well out of earshot. 'Shall I tell you why I'm here?'

'Of course.'

'I came,' he said quietly, 'to express my gratitude, Flora.'

Flora looked at him curiously. 'Really? How mysterious.'

'There's no mystery about it.' His eyes glittered like crystals above the glass-shaded candle between them. 'First, my thanks for handing

Inch Cottage back. As you probably remember, I was in no mood for gratitude the night we parted. Then I gather I have you to thank for a phone call from a certain Mr Beauchamp, asking permission to view my collection of Genista Lyon water-colours.'

'Oh. Marcus got in touch, then.'

A pulse throbbed at the corner of James's mouth. 'He came to Ardlochan to see the paintings last week. He's a friend of yours?'

'Yes,' she said casually, crossing her fingers under the table. 'But I know him in a professional capacity, too. He's putting my sketches of the watchtower on display at the gallery.'

'Congratulations. I'm due in London tomorrow. I'll take a look.' He smiled slowly. 'After all, I do have a proprietorial interest in the subject.'

They looked at each for a long moment.

'Did Marcus offer a good price for the water-colours?' asked Flora at last.

'Astonishingly good. You never hinted at their value, Flora.'

She shrugged. 'You weren't exactly brimming over with sweetness and light at our first couple of meetings, so I kept quiet about them. And afterwards...'

'And afterwards?' he prompted softly.

Flora looked up to meet his eyes very squarely. 'My mind was taken up with other things. I never thought about them again. Besides, I wasn't sure how much the set would fetch, or even if Aunt Jenny's work was still popular. But you're in luck. Her death has upped the market value quite a bit.'

'So I hear.' James smiled. 'I showed Beauchamp the portrait of my grandfather, too——'

'You wouldn't sell that!'

'No,' he said shortly. 'I would not. Whatever you may think of me I've no intention of selling my grandfather. His portrait will hang over the fireplace in the drawing-room of Inch Cottage to impress hotel visitors, as it happens. But Marcus Beauchamp was itching to get his hands on it. Apparently an oil of such quality from an artist known only as a water-colourist would create a lot of interest.'

'Did you show him the portrait of Genista?'

'No, Flora. That's yours.' James stirred his coffee slowly, his face set in harsh lines. 'No doubt you'll be amused to learn I feel bloody beholden to you. It's not something I enjoy.'

'Beholden?'

His eyes darkened as they met hers. 'You were perfectly within your right to hang on to Inch Cottage—so much so that it still feels like yours. I know you handed it back to me, but I can't rid myself of the damnedest feeling that I'm not entitled to it. Even with all the work going on there I keep thinking you'll walk through the kitchen door, or come running down the stairs.' His mouth twisted. 'To hell with Lady Mariotta. The ghost who haunts me is you.'

'Dear me,' said Flora, brusque to mask the turbulence inside her. 'Fey Highland fantasies sound odd coming from you, James Cameron. Besides, the house was really yours all along. Aunt Jenny was just making mischief by passing it over to me.'

His eyes held hers very deliberately. 'Perhaps she envisaged a replay of her own love-affair, with you and me in the leading roles.'

Flora stared at him coldly. 'I hardly think so. Whatever happened between *us* is over, James. Fun while it lasted. But over.' She looked away hastily from the flare of rage in his eyes. 'I must get back.'

They made their way through the still crowded bar, and walked without speaking to James's car. Punctiliously he helped her into the passenger seat, then drove off, the silence unbroken until he turned the car into a lay-by on a quiet stretch of country road.

'Why have you stopped?' asked Flora sharply.

James switched off the lights and half turned in his seat. 'Because there are still things I want to say. And after your parting shot at the table this seems certain to be my only chance.'

'Be quick, then,' she said, in the tone used to hurry up dawdling schoolgirls.

James laughed mirthlessly. 'By all means, schoolma'am. You must put the fear of God in your pupils.'

She gave him a kindling look. 'Please hurry up, James. I must be back before midnight.'

'Still in your role of Cinderella? I just need to make it clear that I wanted you from the start, cottage or no cottage. I only wish I'd had the sense to say so from day one.' He reached out to take her hand, but she snatched it away, terrified that the slightest contact would have her throwing herself into his arms, begging him to hold her close and never let her go.

His fists clenched. 'You don't believe me.'

'Actually, I do,' she said sadly. She knew perfectly well he'd wanted her—and did now, at this very minute, unless she was very much mistaken. But wanting wasn't enough. She wanted him to love her, as Charles Cameron had loved Genista Lyon, with a deep abiding devotion that never died.

'It obviously makes no difference,' he said
bitterly.

'Any difference to what?'

'If you have to ask,' he said with violence,
'what point is there in discussing it? You were
right, it's over. I'll take you back.'

James drove the last few miles to the school
at a speed which frightened Flora to death. He
brought the car to a halt outside the lodge,
jumped out and opened Flora's door, then
jerked her out of her seat and into his arms and
kissed her with a savagery she responded to
helplessly. But almost at once he flung her away
from him, leapt back into the car and drove
off, leaving her standing by the main gates,
breathing raggedly as she watched his tail-lights
vanish from sight. It was a long time before she
climbed into her Mini and drove very slowly up
the drive towards the school, consoling herself
with the thought that it was half-term and she
could go home next day.

Unfortunately her parents had been so taken
with James Cameron that they could talk of
little else when Flora arrived. She had to grit
her teeth and agree, smiling, that he was
charming. Lucy Blair was hard put to hide her
curiosity when she heard Flora had dined with
James when he'd gone to see her at the school.

'Did he want something in particular?' she enquired eagerly.

'Only to thank me. I put the Beauchamp Gallery on to the water-colours Aunt Jenny left him. It seems they offered him a very good price.'

'Oh.' Mrs Blair looked disappointed. 'I thought maybe he'd come to invite you to Scotland again.'

The following Monday Flora was helping her father plant tulip bulbs when Lucy Blair called from an open window, brandishing the phone at her daughter.

Flora rushed into the house to snatch the phone from her mother.

'Hello?' she said eagerly.

'Flora? Marcus Beauchamp.'

Flora slumped down in a chair, burning with disappointment. 'Hello, Marcus.'

After a brief exchange of pleasantries Marcus got down to business. 'Could you possibly dash down here today, Flora? I've sold your set of sketches, but you left one of them unsigned. I'm afraid the client requires a full set of signatures before settling the bill.'

'Oh, right, how careless of me. Fancy someone wanting the whole set!'

Flora gave the glad news to her parents, then hurriedly changed into a brief black skirt and black-braided yellow jacket, brushed her hair into smooth coils on top of her head and rushed downstairs to get in her father's car for a lift to the station. Within a couple of hours she was in the Beauchamp Gallery, basking in a warm welcome from Marcus.

'There's one snag,' said Marcus, as Flora poured coffee from a Georgian silver pot. 'Mr Piper would like you to take the sketches to his hotel in person to add the missing signature. It's only round the corner, shouldn't take you long.'

Flora shrugged, laughing. 'Why not?'

She spent a lively few minutes flirting with Marcus over coffee, then took her leave, feeling a little let down when he saw her off with no suggestion of lunch. Philosophically she walked briskly along through the crowds until she reached the relatively quiet square where Mr Piper's hotel had been catering to visitors for over a century.

She gave her name to the suave young man behind the reception desk, and was immediately directed to a room on the third floor. She was expected, he informed her.

Flora stepped from the lift into a hushed, lushly carpeted corridor and made her way towards room 309. She knocked on the door, smiling politely as it swung open.

'Mr Piper? I'm...' Her jaw dropped as James Cameron took her hand and drew her inside the room.

'Hello, Flora. How beautiful you look.'

CHAPTER ELEVEN

DUMBFOUNDED, Flora allowed James to lead her past the bed to a sofa near the windows, where covered dishes waited on a small table, alongside a frosted bottle in a silver ice-bucket.

'*You're* the client?' Flora said, when she was able to speak.

'Yes.' James removed the cork from the bottle deftly and filled two glasses with champagne. 'After you told me about them I thought it was worth taking a special trip to see them.' He handed her a glass, then took a chair opposite, looking at her steadily. 'I know you don't usually drink wine,' he said, 'but this is exceptionally good. Try it.'

Flora sipped her wine, trying to recover from the shock. 'Why Mr Piper?'

'I was looking at some John Piper screenprints at the gallery when I asked Marcus Beauchamp to conspire with me.'

She looked at him consideringly. 'All very cloak-and-dagger, James.'

'I thought you wouldn't come otherwise.' His eyes were searching. 'Are you angry, Flora?'

'I'm not sure yet,' she said candidly, then smiled a little. 'I hope you paid a good price for the sketches. I need a new car.'

'Too true. The engine sounded rough the other night.' James looked at her sombrely. 'The moment I saw the sketches I knew they were yours. I would have paid whatever price I was asked.'

'Because they're all of Ardlochan?'

'Partly.' James drained his glass. 'Marcus Beauchamp told me he'd also seen the watercolours you did at the watchtower, but you wouldn't put them up for sale.'

'No.' Flora gazed through the window. 'I thought I'd hold on to them as a keepsake. Of the place Aunt Jenny loved so much,' she added.

'I see.'

'Do you?' Flora turned to look at him. 'Or did you imagine I wanted a reminder of my time with you?'

'Why should I think that?' he demanded. 'As you made very clear the other night, in your eyes I'm past history.' He leaned over to remove the silver cover from a plate of sandwiches. 'Smoked salmon—Scottish, naturally.'

Flora helped herself to a plate and a napkin, glad of something to occupy her hands. But to her dismay she found it impossible to swallow the smallest nibble of sandwich and had to resort to champagne to wash it down.

'Shall I ring for something else?' James enquired.

'No! They're delicious.' She flushed slightly. 'I suppose I'm just not hungry.'

'Neither am I.' James topped up their glasses, his eyes holding hers. 'Are you wondering why I asked you here?'

'So I could sign one of the drawings, what else?'

'Not quite.' He leaned back, crossing one long leg over the other. 'When Marcus Beauchamp came to Ardlochan to view the water-colours he looked as though he'd seen a ghost when he met me.'

Flora frowned. 'Why?'

'He'd seen me before.'

'Where?'

'Can't you guess?'

'No. What do you mean?'

'When your sketches were being prepared for display Marcus discovered a few more at the back of your portfolio.'

She stiffened, her colour flaring as the brilliant grey eyes bored into hers. She swallowed some champagne hurriedly. 'I'd forgotten those. I did them that day in the tower, after Catriona went on her merry way.' She shrugged.

'Drawing you over and over, James, was rather like lancing a wound to let the poison out.'

'I could tell,' he said grimly. 'I look like the devil incarnate in all of them—bar one.' He reached down behind his chair, and produced a charcoal drawing.

By the time she'd embarked on this last study of James her mood had changed, as Flora remembered only too well. She stared at the drawing he handed her, wondering how she could have been idiot enough to leave it for James, or anyone else, to see. He was welcome to the others, which were savage caricatures. But this one left the viewer in no doubt as to the artist's feelings towards the subject. James's dark, commanding face had been reproduced with the loving care Genista Lyon had once used to sketch his grandfather.

'Beauchamp was uneasy about letting me have these,' said James. 'I haven't even paid for them yet, by the way.'

'They're not for sale,' said Flora angrily. 'I left them behind by mistake.'

'Do you want them back?'

'No.' Flora made a violent gesture of repudiation. 'Do what you like with them. Tear them up, burn them, for all I care. Just don't insult me by offering money.'

'Does that apply to the watchtower set too?' demanded James, suddenly as angry as Flora.

'No. They were put on sale in the normal way. I'll take your money for those *very* happily!'

They stared at each other malevolently, then James passed a hand over his eyes.

'This is absurd.'

'How right you are,' she retorted, and got up, collecting her handbag. 'If you'll hand over the sketch I'll sign and be on my way.'

James leapt to his feet to stay her, an urgent hand on her wrist. 'Don't. Please.' His eyes narrowed as his fingers found her racing pulse. She tugged, trying to free her hand, but his hand tightened.

'Flora, look at me.'

He put a finger under her resistant chin and raised her face to his, his eyes searching for an instant before he closed them tightly and with a stifled sound seized her in his arms and kissed her so hard that her knees buckled. He held her away at last, his eyes blazing with triumph.

'Now tell me it's over!'

Flora fought free, breathing hard. 'All right! You've proved your point. So the chemistry still works between us——'

'Who the hell cares about that?' he demanded roughly. 'It's not just your body I'm after! I want *you*, Flora Blair, all of you, for always.'

Flora met the glittering grey eyes with scepticism. 'You're joking!'

James threw up his hands in despair. 'God grant me patience—is it something a man's likely to joke about, woman? Maybe they do where you come from, but in my part of the world it's a deadly serious utterance to make! Besides,' he added impatiently, 'why do you think I came chasing after you to that terrifying school of yours?'

'You said you came to thank me,' she reminded him.

'That was just an excuse.' James folded his arms. 'I had some mad idea about taking you by surprise so you'd fall into my arms at first sight of me.'

'If I'd had my first sight of you sooner there'd have been more possibility of it,' she snapped. 'But not much.'

'I thought you'd gone to France.' James's eyes darkened menacingly. 'I made life hell for my mother because I kept picturing you in the Perigord, living it up with lord knows who.'

'Poor Mrs Cameron,' said Flora with sympathy. 'How is she?'

'She sent you her love.' James looked guilty. 'I was supposed to tell you that the other night. I forgot.'

Flora gazed at him speculatively. 'So you thought I was in France until the beginning of term. That, James, was six weeks ago.'

His face set. 'By then I'd persuaded myself I could do without you—that I was the last man to be ruled by his passion for a woman.'

'Your grandfather was.'

'I know.' James stalked over to the window and stood looking out. 'For two whole weeks I persuaded myself I was different—that no woman would be allowed to affect my life in the same way. And with the reconstruction work already underway at Inch Cottage life was hectic enough to convince me I was winning, for a while. Then Marcus Beauchamp contacted me, saying you'd told him about the water-colours, and that was it. One mention of your name and I was back where I started.'

'Which still leaves four weeks,' said Flora relentlessly.

He swung round. 'I would have come then, believe me, but my mother sprained her ankle, and I hadn't the heart to desert her until she was mobile again. Then ten days ago, just as I decided that my mother, Inch Cottage and Ardlochan in general could get on without me, old man MacPhail died.'

'And the laird of Ardlochan had to stay for the funeral,' said Flora quietly. 'I'm sorry. Please give the MacPhails my condolences.'

'Jean seemed to think you'd come back with me and deliver them yourself.' James smiled wryly into Flora's startled eyes. 'Jean has the sight, you understand. Her gift came down through her father's family, undiluted by her English blood.'

Flora shivered slightly. 'She told me I'd go back.'

'And will you?' said James instantly.

She eyed him challengingly. 'In what capacity exactly? I hate to bring it up, but now Inch Cottage is about to change into a hotel you don't have a spare cottage for a mistress any more, unless there's some other little hide-away on your estate.'

James strode towards her and seized her by the elbows, his eyes flaming with anger. 'What the hell are you havering about? I want a wife, not a mistress!'

'It's the first I've heard of it,' she retorted, fighting a violent urge to hurl herself into his arms.

'Then what the devil do you think I was talking about just now?' He shook her until her teeth rattled. 'I've never done it before, so obviously I made a hash of it. I was actually proposing marriage! Why do you think I came charging into that school of yours after you, not to mention getting you here to London on false pretexts, and such nonsense, Flora Blair? Do you honestly think I've ever made such an idiot of myself over a woman before?'

'How do I know?' She glared at him. 'In future take my advice, James Cameron. Make yourself understood more plainly if you go round proposing to anyone else.'

The animation drained from his face as he let her go. 'There's no fear of that,' he said bitterly. 'You've just been witness to my first and last proposal to any woman.'

Flora eyed him narrowly, something in the proud jut of James Cameron's chin telling her he meant exactly what he said. 'In that case,' she said meekly, 'I accept.'

James stood very still. Flora smiled at him uncertainly, his frozen expression giving her no clue to his reaction.

'Would you say that again?' he said at last.

'No, I will not,' she said crossly. 'If you won't propose again why should I accept twice?'

He pounced, jerking her into his arms, and began kissing her feverishly, muttering endearments between the kisses as he picked her up and sat down with her in his lap. Flora abandoned herself to the kisses and caresses with an all-out enthusiasm which put an end to any conversation for some time until James said something which made her push away his restraining arms.

'Wait!' she ordered breathlessly. 'What did you just say?'

James thrust a hand through his tousled hair, blinking. 'I was kissing you, not talking, *mo cridhe.*'

Flora bit her lip, suddenly sure she'd imagined it.

James's eyes lit with an unholy light. 'Unless,' he said casually, 'you heard me saying I love you.'

Her face flamed. 'If I did, it was like your proposal—hard to recognize!'

He frowned. 'But Flora, my darling girl, what else have I been saying all along?'

'You've never mentioned love. All you ever said was that you wanted me.'

'Then to avoid all possible confusion——' James raised both her hands to his lips and kissed them in turn. 'I love you, Flora Blair, and I'm asking you to be my wife. Am I making myself clear?'

'As a bell,' she assured him and reached up to kiss him.

He shook her gently. 'I was beginning to think I should have left you up in that tower until you said yes.'

'It would have saved a lot of misery on my part if you had,' she said, sighing.

'Were you really so unhappy?' he asked in a tone of such tenderness that Flora melted against him, nodding wordlessly.

'And are you willing to spend the rest of your life at Ardlochan with me?' he went on after a lengthy interval.

'After I've worked the necessary notice at the school—— Don't scowl like that; I can't walk out mid-term!'

James conceded the point reluctantly. 'My mother said you wouldn't.'

Flora's eyes narrowed. 'She knew what you had in mind, then?'

He laughed, shifting her more comfortably on his lap. 'She told me to swallow my pride and stop behaving like a great gowk.'

Flora giggled. 'I do like your mother. I hope she won't mind sharing a house with me.'

'The question doesn't arise.' He grinned. 'Part of my mother's impatience to see me married is a burning desire to live in Edinburgh near her greatest friend. She's wanted to for years, I discover, but hadn't the heart to desert me.'

Flora sat up straight. 'Ah! Now I see it all. Your only motive for marrying me is to get someone to look after you.'

'If that were so I'd make do with Agnes MacPhail,' he retorted.

'She cooks better than I do!'

'You have other attributes I value more.'

She fluttered her eyelashes. 'Such as?'

'If I go bankrupt I can live on your earnings as an artist,' he said promptly, then, laughing, stifled her indignant protests with a kiss, and pulled her to her feet. 'Come on. Time to go.'

'Where?' said Flora, casting a wistful eye at the bed. 'I thought you were going to make mad, passionate love to me now I'm officially yours.'

James heaved a great sigh. 'I'd like to.' He looked at his watch. 'But if we stay even a few minutes longer I'll have to pay for this room for another day, and, believe me, it costs an arm and a leg. I've just bought a very expensive set of sketches, remember, not to mention the expense of my approaching plunge into matrimony.'

'And they said romance was dead!' jeered Flora.

His smile took her breath away. 'Flora, if I take you to bed now we're likely to stay there until tomorrow. And we can't. I've rung your parents to say we'll be with them this afternoon.'

'You were taking me for granted a bit!'

'Not once I'd seen my portrait.' James kissed her lingeringly. 'The moment I set eyes on it I knew how you felt about me whether you admitted it or not. So let's away to Gloucestershire, where I shall ask your father to give me his daughter, then we'll ring my mother and give her the glad news. Afterwards we take your parents out for a meal and wallow in wedding plans, then tomorrow I'm taking you back to Ardlochan for the rest of half term.'

'Don't I get a say in all this?' she demanded, laughing.

'You said everything necessary when you accepted my proposal, Flora Blair,' he said firmly. 'I think your aunt Jenny would be pleased.'

Flora nodded. 'It's probably exactly what she had in mind when she sent me chasing off to see her love-nest. She probably hoped that bedroom of theirs would give you ideas——' She blushed scarlet suddenly. 'Not, of course, that she had any idea I'd invite you into it.'

'Of course not,' said James, straight-faced.

Flora gave him an indignant dig in the ribs, chuckling. 'I bet she's up there somewhere with your grandfather, gloating over the way things turned out.'

'If so I imagine she wasn't too pleased about her darling Flora's imprisonment in the watch-tower!' James eyed her, grinning. 'By the way you can wreak your revenge by leaving Catriona Urquhart off the guest-list for the wedding.'

Flora smiled rapturously as he closed the door behind them. 'Not on your life! I want her there. All the revenge I'll ever need is a walk down the aisle with you, nodding graciously at her as we pass.'

He caught her by the hand. 'Is that your only motive for marrying me?'

'Goodness, no, James! For one thing I madly fancy a bridegroom in a kilt. And for another I'm not getting any younger. I felt I'd better accept your proposal before my charms began to fade—— Hey!' she added breathlessly, as he swept her into the lift and began shaking her. 'Don't you want to hear the third reason?'

'I hope,' said James forcefully, 'that you're about to say you can't live without me. That, my dear Miss Blair, is why I'm marrying *you*.'

Flora moved closer, suddenly in deadly earnest. 'But that's it exactly, James—the precise reason why I said yes. I've had a couple of months of trying to live without you and hated every minute of it.'

James pulled her close and kissed her. 'In that case,' he muttered against her lips, 'I'm warning you now. For the rest of your days you're never going to be parted from me a minute longer than I can help.' He kissed her again. 'Not to mention the nights,' he added, and reached behind him to press the button which took the lift to the top floor again, winning him a few more moments of privacy to remove any last, lingering doubts Flora might have harboured on the subject.

'By the way,' said James, grinning, when they finally emerged from the hotel, 'in the circumstances couldn't you see your way clear to knocking a bit off the price I'm paying Marcus Beauchamp for your drawings?'

'Certainly not!' Flora tucked a hand through his arm jauntily. 'You'll value them all the more for having paid the going rate for a set of Flora Blair masterpieces. There won't be any more.'

James stopped dead on the pavement. 'Why not? There's nothing to stop you drawing and painting to your heart's content after we're married.'

'But by then my name will be Cameron, remember. The only one in the world to possess an original Flora Blair is you, James!'

The Gloucestershire village of Flora's birth had rarely been witness to a more picturesque occasion than the Blair-Cameron wedding. After a week of gales and snow showers the weather relented to provide a brilliantly sunny January day, leaving a faint powdering of snow to provide the perfect backdrop for the photographs taken outside the small Norman church. Edward Blair radiated pride as he escorted his daughter down the aisle, the bride a vision in her ivory silk dress, with ivy trailing from her bouquet of roses and lilies, and entwined in the coronet of fresh flowers in her hair. The bride groom and best man, waiting at the altar, looked so handsome in their kilts that there were sentimental sighs from every female guest present as James Charles Cameron took Flora Genista Blair to his lawful wedded wife in a church full of sunshine and flowers and music as the choir sang 'O, my luve is like a red red rose', in deference to the Scottish contingent before giving a more conventional Bach encore. And afterwards as the guests hurled confetti at the happy pair outside the church gate a piper in full ceremonial uniform provided the finishing touch by seeing them off to the wedding breakfast to the stirring strains of 'Scotland the Brave'.

'I did so enjoy my wedding day,' said Flora happily as they drove north next day.

'I did too. Though I enjoyed my wedding night even more,' added James with a wicked grin.

'I'm so glad you were pleased,' said Flora primly, then chuckled. 'Did you see Catriona's face at the reception? You'd have thought she was drinking vinegar, not champagne. Though you have to hand it to her,' she added fairly, 'I think she was rather brave to turn up at all.'

'Pride. We Scots are like that.'

'Effrontery I'd call it! After that shabby trick she played it's lucky I didn't clobber her with

my bouquet yesterday—though I must admi
she looked fantastic in that amazing scarlet hat.

'I didn't notice; I was too taken up witl
looking at you.'

Flora gave her husband a melting glance. 'I'n
glad. All that trouble I took to look my bes
was just for you, James.'

He reached out a hand to grasp hers for a
moment. 'By the way, you haven't said a word
about the lack of wedding gift from you
bridegroom.'

'I don't need one, James. Mother gave me
the triple row of pearls Aunt Jenny left her, sc
I don't need jewellery, and otherwise I have
everything in the world I could possibly want.

'I knew there was a good reason for mar
rying you!' James laughed, then cast a smug
look at her. 'Nevertheless there is a wedding
present waiting for you at Ardlochan.'

'What is it?' demanded Flora, eyes sparkling

'Wait and see.'

'Oh, James, don't be maddening. Give me a
hint.'

'Certainly not.'

'It's a dog!'

'No. We've got a couple of those already, re
member.' And not a word more would James
utter on the subject for the rest of the journey
no matter what entreaties Flora made.

It was late when they arrived at Ardlochan.

'Pity it's dark,' remarked Flora, yawning. 'We could have stopped to look at the progress on Inch Cottage.'

'Not tonight,' said James firmly. 'For the moment all I can think of is dinner and bed—though not necessarily in that order.'

When they arrived at the house lights were blazing from the main windows. Before the car stopped the great front door flew open in welcome and Agnes MacPhail, followed by Jean and Donald, came hurrying to welcome the laird and his bride home. There was much congratulating and kissing and handshaking, then James delighted the ladies, Flora included, by carrying his bride across the threshold, through the great hall and on into the morning-room before setting Flora on her feet.

Flora gave a crow of delight as she took in the freshly painted walls and charming new curtains, then her smile faded and she stood very still as she saw the group of water-colours hung on the rear wall of the room, well away from direct light.

She spun round to face James, her eyes incredulous. 'But I thought you sold Aunt Jenny's paintings to Marcus!'

'I told you he offered me a good price. I didn't say I accepted it.' He took her in his arms, rubbing his cheek against her hair.

'Charles Edward Cameron would come back to haunt me if I sold his beloved Genista's masterpieces.'

'Oh, James,' said Flora, sniffing inelegantly. 'They're the loveliest wedding present any one ever had—and the room, too; it's perfect. Did you choose the colours?'

'No. My lady mother did that. She said the room was about ten years overdue for a lick of paint, and hoped you'd like it, but if you didn't she wouldn't be in the least offended.'

'I love it!' Flora assured him.

'Good. But my gift is nothing to do with paintings, Mrs Cameron. Agnes says you're to wash your hands down here and come and eat right away or the meal will spoil. You can have your present later.'

'But I'm dying to know what it is!' complained Flora, as she went off to do Agnes's bidding. 'I'll never survive until after dinner.'

Despite her curiosity it was late by the time the celebration meal was over and the three MacPhails were gone at last. It was midnight before James escorted his bride up the imposing stairs to bed.

'Right—now it's time for my present. By the way, you haven't told me where we're to sleep,' Flora said, yawning. 'Do I just move into your room? Or is there some grand master bedroom where the laird of Ardlochan always brings his bride?'

'My old room's a bit spartan, and the master bedroom hasn't been touched since my grand-mother slept there. Alone. I've always disliked it, so I thought we'd redecorate it eventually for visitors. We're sleeping in the west tower.'

Something in his voice narrowed Flora's eyes as she let him pull her along the upper gallery. 'Sounds very grand, James. I hope it's not too cold and cavernous. I remember the room Catriona took me to the night I came to dinner. Like a fridge with a four-poster. I was shivering so much I couldn't put my lipstick on straight.'

'The master bedroom, without doubt. I don't think you'll find this one too bad,' said James and threw open a door with a flourish. 'There you are, Mistress Cameron. Your wedding gift.'

Flora stood on the threshold, staring wildly at the flower-wreathed carpet, the swagged, flamboyant curtains and gilded paintwork, the *chaise-longue* piled with silk cushions. And dominating them all the familiar brass bed. Suddenly her eyes overflowed with tears and she hurled herself into her husband's arms, locking her arms round his neck kissing him over and over again.

'Oh, James, what a glorious, wonderful thing to do!'

He let out a great sigh of relief. 'Thank the lord you like it. The decorators, not to mention my mother, thought I was totally insane. Mother, who never had a qualm about doing up the morning-room, was adamant that I should have consulted you first about this, but I wanted to surprise you.'

'You did, you did!' Flora danced round the room, all her travel-weariness forgotten as she patted cushions and fingered the brocade of the curtains. 'But this is all new, James—how on earth did you manage to get it all the same?'

'With enormous difficulty! The only things to survive from Inch Cottage are the ornaments and the furniture. The curtains and carpet were too ancient to transfer even if they'd have fitted, so I had to search far and wide before I found replacements. Are you pleased, *mo cridhe*?' he asked, holding out his arms.

Flora ran to him, holding up a face so radiant that he was left in no doubt as to her answer. 'And does that door mean a bathroom with gold dolphins and mirrors on the wall?'

'Of course, not to mention towels sporting oak leaves and sprays of broom.'

'I always meant to ask about that, James. The broom was for Genista, of course, but why the oak leaf?'

'It's the plant badge of the Camerons, you beautiful, ignorant Sassenach,' he said, holding her close.

Flora sighed. 'How romantic. He really loved her, didn't he?'

'No more,' said James, suddenly in total earnest, 'than I love you, Flora Cameron.'

A long time later, in the warm, blissful aftermath of their lovemaking, Flora turned her head on James's shoulder in the depths of the great brass bed, and gazed about her at the voluptuous, softly lit room.

'Now I come to think of it there's something missing, James. Where's the drawing of your grandfather?'

'Downstairs in my study, where he belongs.' He propped himself up on an elbow, smiling down at her possessively. 'The only man allowed in *this* room, *mo cridhe*, is me.'